AUTOPSY OF AN ENGINE

Autopsy of an Engine

AND OTHER STORIES FROM THE CADILLAC PLANT

Lolita Hernandez

COFFEE HOUSE PRESS
2004

Coffee House Press books are available to the trade through our primary distributor, Consortium Book Sales & Distribution, 1045 Westgate Drive, Saint Paul, MN 55114. For personal orders, catalogs, or other information, write to: Coffee House Press, 27 North Fourth Street, Suite 400, Minneapolis, MN 55401.

Coffee House Press is a nonprofit literary publishing house. Support from private foundations, corporate giving programs, government programs, and generous individuals help make the publication of our books possible. We gratefully acknowledge their support in detail in the back of this book. To you and our many readers across the country, we send our thanks for your continuing support.

LIBRARY OF CONGRESS CIP DATA

Hernandez, Lolita, 1947–
Autopsy of an engine and other stories from the Cadillac plant/by Lolita Hernandez.
p. cm.
ISBN 1-56689-161-2 (alk. paper)
1. Cadillac automobile—Fiction. 2. Automobile industry and trade—Fiction. 3. Automobile industry workers—Fiction. 4. Automobile factories—Fiction. 5. Detroit (Mich.)—Fiction. I. Title.
PS3608.E767A97 2004
813'.6—DC22
2004012787

FIRST EDITION | FIRST PRINTING
1 3 5 7 9 8 6 4 2
Printed in Canada

for Pedro and Demecina

Contents

Closing the Cadillac Plant

The final closing of Cadillac Motor Car Company's Clark Street facility in Detroit was an astonishing, bewildering, confounding, dumbfounding event that approached languidly as if a dream and concluded like the biting slap of subzero windchill. On one level, it was like experiencing orange marmalade for the first time. You eat eat eat the sticky sweet until a long strand of bitter rind wraps around your tongue and you discover that this is marmalade, not jam or preserves. Then again it was like walking along a beach at dawn on a Sunday morning and finding a starfish. Or like strolling through a beautiful graveyard, Elmwood Cemetery on Mt. Elliot, for example, and stumbling upon a dead body. An old man's dead body. A body that was already rotting.

Cadillac Motor Car Company, once the oldest automobile manufacturer in the city, began its Clark Street assembly operations in 1927. Then considered the most modern automobile complex in the world, Clark Street jointly produced cars with Fleetwood, which supplied the bodies from its Fort Street plant. At its peak in the mid-seventies, nearly 10,000 people worked on Clark Street, which by then boasted of a foundry, plating operation, engineering facility, warehouse, and waste treatment center. The foundry moved to Ohio in the mid-sixties. The motor line left for Livonia in 1979, marking the real beginning of the end for the facility. The final car assembly line shut down in December 1987, and moved to Arlington, Texas. Plating discontinued operations in March 1993. Engineering's closing in March 1994 marked the official shuttering of the Clark Street site.

The process of shutdown between December 1992 and March 1994 was happy and sad, a laugh and a cry—all at once. A time to remember and reflect on the past, also a time to forget about everything and move on. That was how confusing the final months at Clark Street were. For sure it was bitter seeing the insides of the Cadillac buildings ripped apart department by department, fixture by fixture, pipe by pipe. The place had been a jumping hulk of a factory full of live sweaty bodies in its heyday. Now it would become a 1927 dinosaur loaded only with spirit echoes of people who used to wrestle those Caddies into existence, blow them off the blueprint, and sweet-talk them off the line like you sweet-talk love on a Saturday night.

This is how the complex was set up. Clark Street was the main happening street. On Clark you could look up and see all the variations of Cadillac World Headquarters logos that marked the area as General Motors, Cadillac territory. Michigan Avenue bordered the north, Brandon on the south, Vinewood the east and Junction the west. Cadillac marine blue and plain white formed the background for little red beakless legless merlette ducks on the Cadillac shields strategically placed on Clark Street. The front entrances to the manufacturing building, final assembly, and the administration building were located on Clark.

People used to be thick on that street, especially in the summer at lunchtime. On a summer day you could see them sitting on the curbs, the administration building ledges, under shade trees. They were cooling off, discussing line speeds or department gossip; they were waiting to return to those big, beautiful, shiny Caddies. How people loved to say that they built Cadillacs, the flagship of the corporation, the ultimate luxury car of the nation. How people loved to let the name Cadillac roll off their tongues the way those babies rolled off the line. But the pain to build them: in the pits, like sardines on the motor line, frying from sparks in welding, eaten alive by chemicals in plating.

The Engineering building was situated on Scotten Avenue at the southeastern edge of the Cadillac complex, behind Clark. Scotten Avenue was different from Clark. Nothing livened up that street even though the back entrance to the final assembly building on Scotten was the entrance of choice for many workers. When final assembly left, Clark and Scotten became ghost streets, except for some administrative offices, the Engineering building, and an assortment of electricians, pipe fitters, and millwrights still scattered throughout the facility.

Months before GM closed the Cadillac Engineering building, the complex buzzed with activity. Prior to that, at least since final assembly moved, the pace had been slow, dreamy, almost lethargic. As long as the Engineering building remained open, those working there could fool themselves into thinking that Clark Street was still alive. There was still hope that it could rouse like Jack's giant. After the announcement that Engineering would close, everyone woke up from their somnambulation and realized they were facing a gigantic task. Everything movable had to go. Every usable chair, desk, and computer scattered throughout the site had to be crated, hauled to a staging dock, and shipped to a new GM location. Equipment destined to remain in service was packed and crated off to other GM facilities after managers from Clark Street haggled with managers from other sites over placement of presses or bed plates or giant instruments for precision measuring. They took pictures of everything. You would have thought they were conducting a flea market or fire sale.

What was not worth saving got chucked. Everything not embedded in the bricks, bolted to the floors, or locked into the lanes of steam pipes and electrical conduits that traversed the ceilings was thrown into big and little disposal containers: metal into c-five pans, reams of confidential reports from the Engineering building archives into large dumpsters called gondolas. Buckets of old bolts and automotive whatnots from the Merritt Street Warehouse and from the Engineering stockroom sounded merry and tinkling as they knocked past ancient tailpipes to arrive at the bottom of c-five pans. Crews of skilled trades maintenance teams salvaged copper and steel, which the company sold as scrap.

The process for distributing the workers, hourly and salary, to other GM facilities or to the streets wasn't any neater. For months while they cleaned the place up, Cadillac workers didn't know their future with the corporation. Fewer still knew the future of the buildings. The wrecking ball? New industrial occupants? Vagrants had already taken up residence. They quickly familiarized themselves with the hot and cold water in the showers. They had already picked out the desirable sleeping spots. As the vagrants were settling in, the people who worked at Cadillac Clark Street were swinging out in a curious combination of denial and nostalgia.

Whatever the outcome everyone, hourly and salary workers alike, hurled themselves into the process of closure. It consumed them. They ate and slept it. Sort and discard, pack and save. The more and more it was stripped, that grand old behemoth, five-storied, 1920s self-contained miracle of production began to resemble an old gypsy queen, dancing around a campfire. Slow and haphazard at first, a tease. Yes, there is still life in me. Look, they are painting my walls. Look, they are tending my front lawns. Look, they have ordered new equipment. Believe in me; believe in magic. And then her eyes turn ashy white. She gives you a maddening seductive look, riveting your eyes. Just when you are ready to believe: pack up fools, she says, the jig is up.

That's when the orgy began, one orgasmic slam after another of fixtures and furniture into gondolas and c-five pans. It got wild in there. Pretty soon people organized into teams in order to search through trash for usable keepsakes. There were the loners who scurried from floor to floor, dumpster to dumpster, finding treasures: a manometer no longer used to measure pressure, a bar of steel, an assortment of u-joints, a bicentennial manufacturer's plate. There were those who scavenged handfuls of bolts and nuts, wires and braces. They could be seen shuffling them around on their benches as if they were the only thing they had control over: bits and pieces of the past that they had saved.

Moving out of a factory as big as Cadillac takes years of planning and packing. It takes years of rolling up lines, ripping down conveyors, and gradually carting off a machine or two on flatbed semis. It isn't like moving from the home where you raised your children to a retirement condominium—a load of plants in one car trip, a load of odds and ends, pots and pans in another. You need helicopters and skyhooks and helium balloons to move a factory. That was how the Cadillac smokestacks left the site that July day in 1993.

It was sheer magic. The workmen cut a hole in the side of each stack through which they placed a balloon with a fishing line attached. The balloon ascended to the top of the stack, then descended over the side of the smokestack shortly after, because the workmen had made a pinhole in each balloon. Then sturdier cable was attached to the nylon starter cable, pulled through, and clamped off. The skyhook was summoned. Time is money with a skyhook. A skyhook isn't a U-Haul. Three minutes per stack from placement of lift cable to liftoff from a Cadillac plant roof. Three minutes times eighty-six stacks and all the belch and steam of sixty-seven years of Cadillac production on Clark Street was over.

One man, arriving at the desperate realization that his impending layoff could affect making payments on his 1992 Sedan de Ville, contracted his car and himself as driver to several of the small funeral homes in the city. So with a flick of the wrist and minimal expenditure, Paradise, as we called him, converted his Caddie—gray on gray in gray, sleek as an eel and sweet-smelling on the inside like drugstore faux designer colognes—into a rental funeral car by adding a box of pink Puffs tissues. For the ladies, he said. They are always the ones to cry. Besides, the pink looks good on gray. "Hey," he said, "they may close this plant, but I'm going to keep me a Cadillac car."

If you have a mother or father dying slowly, you see them diminish. The end is coming; you should be prepared. But when your loved one crosses that nodal line from which there is no return, you are still in shock. You still grieve.

What should the preacher say then? Be kind to the family for they are grieving and need their strength. Should the priest say: the soul of the dearly departed has risen and is in the lap of the Lord? Take comfort in that, my children?

Or should we, the children of that big-lapped Cadillac mama say: ¡Adiós!, Viejita! You were one baaad, baaad, baaad mamajama.

This collection of twelve stories is my adiós. The stories are fictional, but I tried my best to make them reflect the real life of the plant. Of course, when I wanted them to reflect exact con-versations, exact thought patterns, exact time progressions I would get into trouble. The stories would fall flat. They would represent nothing but my tired nostalgia. They wouldn't do what I myself needed. They wouldn't answer for me the all-important question: why was I working in a factory? I wouldn't discover one single thing about why any of us were there.

That was the main question the weekly paycheck couldn't quite answer. So I found myself consulting with my proletar-ian ancestors. The ones I swore were hovering above me as I shot number one piston. When I walked back to visit on the block line or in the cam department or upstairs in piston assembly, I could feel the weight of all the years of people doing the same thing in the same place for the same reason. As far as I could figure, that was my real family: the living and the dead in that place. They are in these stories. Them and me. We were all fabricating more than painted hunks of steel that could go honk honk honk in that rich melodic Cadillac way and then hog up the highways, humming away like we used to on the lines. Hummm.

L. H.

Detroit, 1994, revised 2004

This Is Our Song for Today

Years of solitude had taught him that in one's memory,
all days tend to be the same, but that there is not a day,
not even in jail or in the hospital,
which does not bring surprises,
which is not a translucent network of minimal surprises.
—JORGE LUIS BORGES, *The Waiting*

Firefly

When the first engine for the day arrived in front of the man whose job was to put the water pump and front cover on it, he opened his mouth as wide as the great Mississippi River in the days before debris narrowed its flow and out spilled his tenor's tongue in song: *Firefly, ooh ooh firefly*. Clear and mellow like raindrops on an emerald leaf. *Shine your light tonight*. With his goatee aimed at the network of air hoses dangling over his job, he crinkled the chocolate skin over his high cheekbones and squeezed his eyes into a thin, wavy line as if those facial contortions could help propel his song. *Assist the moon and stars in helping us to ease our minds*. A Temptations song he heard on the radio on the way to work followed him from the Clark Street parking lot and escorted him to his station on motor line number one. The song settled in his chest then escaped through his arms the first time they stretched to place a front plate cover on an engine. The song curved his body over the creeping engine as if caressing a microphone: *Firefly, ooh ooh firefly*. With his hips swiveling in one direction, his shoulders swaying in another, he eased a cover onto each engine. Thuupp. Yeah. *Golden light of serenity*.

He was so absorbed with the song's mellifluous notes that he didn't notice them slip from his mouth and enter the linkage of the conveyor each time he stepped up to an engine. They snaked to the end of the line and rolled under the surface, clinging to the oily mixture of trash and garbage that traveled the conveyor. They resurfaced at the head of the line for the return trip to his water pump job. At a rate of eighty contacts with an engine an hour, by midmorning the entire half-city block of piston line was running like warm grease. Instead of the normal clank, clank, clank, the line flowed with a phlump, phlump, phlump. *Firefly. Hmmmm, hmmmm, phlump. Hmmmm, hmmmm, phlump.*

His job was located just after the midsection of the line, past the frantic team of eight noisy young men who installed pistons. He had been elbow to elbow with them in the middle of the pistons until two weeks ago, when the cover job opened. When he worked pistons he couldn't hear himself think. He hummed blues songs so low and deep that he didn't need words to know what he was saying to himself. He went so deep inside himself that he managed to block out the environment around him. He erased the cussing, the fighting, the drinking.

After shuffling from heavy job to sweaty job in his twelve years at Cadillac, at age thirty he had landed in a spot where low conversational buzzing predominated and he could wear designer jeans to work. He was a world away from the chaos of the densely-peopled piston section at the head of the line. He was now in the middle of nothing but small talk, punctuated by the blips, braaps, and wiiirngs of an assortment of bolt-tightening air guns and the incessant clank, clank, clank of the conveyor. At the end of the line the murmur of human conversation blended with the metallic sounds of production and became part of the assembly noise.

Hmmmm, hmmmm, phlump. Hmmmm, hmmmm, phlump. Musical notes wound themselves around the timing chain, slithered over and around the cam lobes, caressed the crank throws before he sealed them in the engine with the front cover. Those engines were destined to hum and purr once they reached the road. He looked around him and saw the sleepy, contented smiles of the women who worked nearby. Their hands seemed to float from bolt trays to engines to air guns as if in a dream. The engine repair man at the end of the line leaned against his empty bench, nodding with relief at each healthy engine that passed in front of him. The man on the last job lifted each engine from the line with the transfer turnover then waltzed it to its place on a hanging conveyor destined for line two.

To its singer, the notes of the song, "Firefly," became a source of power he never knew he could have. He began moving his body as if it were a baton orchestrating all the operations of the line, even those at its head; he had remote control through the notes riding the links of the conveyor.

He surveyed his territory and spotted the quiet woman whose eyes almost never left the timing chains she installed. That's when he marched a few steps up the line to rouse her, bring her into his choir. He crooned, *Shine your light naturally,* and she looked up in confusion as if she had been yanked from another world. He instructed her, Open your mouth in a perfect circle and sing, *Firefly, ooh ooh firefly.* He demonstrated. *Firefly,* it's our song for today. I can teach it to you. She fixed her dark eyes on him and obediently formed her mouth into an o but before a note could fall out, the laughter of shyness overtook her. He returned to his job disgusted and quiet, unaware that it was her nature to be embarrassed by direct human contact.

A few engines later he was relieved for his first break. Before leaving the line he threw one last bar of song over his shoulder. *I shouldn't have to lie to make it seem all right.* The lady on the timing chain job began her own soft humming. She smiled, amazed that a Monday morning on line number one could begin with a song.

Pajarillo, Pajarillo

If she put her ear up to the line after each engine passed her station, she could hear a faint chirp. At first she thought it was one of the many birds who became trapped inside the factory and frantically flew high in the rafters looking for a way out, but, of course, rarely found one. There was no way out up above the lines; only at the edges of the entire floor were there windows. But even if a little bird could figure a way out by flying low and straight, it would still have to worry about passing through all the machinery in the cam department or all the lines and washers in the block department. Even if it reached as far as the head line, things were so thick over there who knew what could happen to a little bird. When a bird was no longer seen, everyone hoped that it had escaped through the loading dock area, but knew it had probably become weak and hungry and had fallen into the line and been carried away by the links in the conveyor to the pit underneath. She figured that every year at the beginning of summer when the cleaners removed the sludge build-up under the line, they must see a bushel or two of dead oily birds.

She looked up every time she heard a chirp, thinking it was an echo from real birds flying above her. Seeing none, she suspected that the chirps arose from the spirits of the birds whose bodies dropped off the conveyor at her section because the sludge had lost its hold on them. They were calling out to her.

No one else heard chirps in the line. She began to sing to them softly *pajarillo, pajarillo; qué bonitos ojos tienes* and a bird would answer back with a chirp. Sometimes she jiggled her timing chain over the line because she thought the jingling sounded like their muffled chirping. *Lástima que tengas dueño.*

She worked her eight hours with her head bowed, leaning into the line not to miss any chirps. For this reason she had developed few friends in the factory. No one came to visit her where she worked because she gave the appearance of being a loner or afraid of people. However, her coworkers didn't consider her arrogant, because her stooped, rounded shoulders and her bowed head (even when she was walking to the bathroom or getting a cup of coffee from the machine) made her look humble. Many of them realized that she was just plain shy and that she didn't speak much English. Her smile, when she cocked her head to respond to a greeting, was wide and toothy.

She had learned the song from her mother, who had died many years before in her hometown of Agualeguas, Mexico. Her mother had sung the same few words (*nada mas*) when washing the dishes or especially when making the tortillitas. *Pajarillo, pajarillo. Qué bonitos ojos tienes. Lástima que tengas dueño.* Her mother never tired of singing the same words over and over, which was a good thing because now it is the only song of her mother's she can remember. She had almost forgotten about it until the first time she heard a chirp in the line.

Turn Me 'Round

An engine block fell off the line one hour before lunch. It jumped off the light blue, oil-stained stand on the conveyor; it thumpa, thumpa, thumpa'd itself away from the exact spot programmed for it by the broadcast system; it bugalooed its way from its spot between the block in front of it that was scheduled for a green Brougham and the one behind it, slated for a brown Sedan de Ville. It tumbled onto the wooden floorboard of the even side of the piston section as if refusing that sweet yellow Eldorado waiting for it across the street in final assembly.

The instant before it began its fall from the line, all eight of the men who installed pistons converged on the block: the installers of even pistons buzzed on one side, the odds on the other. Some indistinct cackling, snorting, and guffawing emerged from the cluster, which began to sound like a barnyard opera. Then in one fluid motion, the group reeled backwards. Someone shouted: *heave ho, muthafucka* and the block flew off the stand.

The way any block sat on the conveyor, it would have to wiggle considerably to escape the specially constructed stand that cradled its top corners. All blocks rode upside down on line number one in order to facilitate piston installation. You could lean against one and it wouldn't budge. You could turn the crank when the crank was tight and there were four or five pistons in the block and the block would stay solid on the conveyor. You could take a big torque wrench or a hammer or a piston tray or anything and knock it against the block and it wouldn't move.

A block was lightweight on line one, relatively speaking. It emerged hollow from the washer at the head of the line: a scooped-out section for the crank, a tunnel for the cam, eight empty cylinders for the pistons. It became an engine on its way down the line to meet the crank, pistons, timing chain, water pump, crank pulley, oil pump and pan. By the end of the line, a block was an engine, ready to receive the plumbing and electrical parts on lines two and three.

Actually, a block crossed into the realm of engine after the crank and pistons were in place. At the moment the block scheduled for the yellow Eldorado left its stand on the conveyor, it had a crank and four pistons in it. It was caught in the middle of its transformation, half engine, half block.

This is how it happened. First its rear lifted to the left, then the front right bank followed suit and shifted. When the front shifted, the engine block began a tumble that would put the front facedown and the left bank straight up in the air.

At the same moment that the engine block touched the side of the line in the first stages of tumble, the woman on the oil pan tightening job, the second to the last station on the line, threw her gray head back, closed her baby blue eyes, lifted her flabby pale white arms, and belted out in a voice as loud and definite as a backfire, *Ain't gonna let nobody turn me 'round, turn me 'round, turn me 'round.*

It only *seemed* as if her voice rang out in accompaniment of the block's descent. But she had no knowledge at all of events in the piston area. Her station was far enough away that she could barely see the group there; they neither saw her head bob back and forth in time to the melody nor heard her militant tune. In vain, the previous day she had conducted a one-woman protest against redistribution of work on the line. An extra stud had trickled down from a station higher up and landed on her job. An agreement between union and management a week before had doomed her struggle, but she continued it with song, under the watchful eye of the foreman who was camping on her job, hoping to intimidate her into silence. He didn't want her to rile the others. *I'm gonna keep on walkin', keep on talkin', till they change this goddam job.*

Next the engine disengaged completely from the stand in a one-hundred-eighty-degree flip. For an instant the engine was right-side up, front forward, precariously supported by the edge of the line and a supply tray of rod nuts attached to it.

All weekend long she had brooded over the changes on her job. *Ain't gonna let nobody turn me 'round.*

Any Friday afternoon, that engine could have been the victim of reefer and bourbon. But that Monday morning it fell for eight reasons lost in the relentless clicking, clacking, clanking, whirring, buzzing, body-bumping-body, sweating, spitting that seemed to be the real business of the piston line.

It was when the engine was in its final stage of falling that the woman who installed the timing chain at a station almost exactly in the center of the line, also heard the strains of melodic resistance. In her left ear there was music, in her right the cacophony from the piston area. Through her body the two unrelated phenomena became one.

So just at the moment that the engine flipped another one-hundred-eighty-degrees, bumped against the edge of the tray that had briefly supported it, and landed on the floorboard, the timing chain lady heard *Turn me 'round, turn me 'round, turn me 'round.*

Then the engine crashed, BOODOOM, creating a hole in the floorboard where number six piston installer normally stood. Two men picked up the engine with their hands and reloaded it singing *heave ho.*

The timing chain lady looked straight ahead at a tray of pistons coming from the second floor on the overhead conveyor and wondered if they would see the inside of an engine that day. To her left the singing lady argued with the foreman, who was completely unaware of the fallen engine. To her right, number six installer was dancing around the hole in the floorboard in an effort to load his piston into the engine designated for the brown Sedan de Ville.

Jumbie Jamboree

The woman who checked the piston rings observed the panorama of craziness up and down the line from her sub-assembly station. She said to herself *oui foote we making real bacchanal here today* as she lifted number one piston from the tray in front of her. She twirled its rings to check for damage and strained to hear the tinny tinkling of the rings slapping in their grooves. They sounded light and airy next to the thumping and all the jumping up and down from the thin young men behind her. She was always back to back bottom to bottom with the whole piston crew as she shuffled from end to end of her eight-foot zone. That short stretch didn't give her enough exercise to shake off the bowls of pelau she brought for lunch each day. So she grew big and bufootoo, as they would say in her native Trinidad, and every day found her dancing cheek to cheek with some slim young man shooting the same pistons she had checked. *Oui foote.* These days her arms hung wide by her side, not close to her heart, and her breasts nestled in her lap like the three children she left back home when she came to this country to get a job so she could feed them because her husband had left her and gone to another island. She told some of her coworkers—*He went to Cuba. At least that's what they said, but who knows. Men these days travel however they want.*

Just like these foolish young men run up and down this line when they get a little bit of brown juice in them.

It wasn't bourbon that possessed them that morning before lunch, before the week had finished waking up, even though an engine jumped off the line as if it already had juice and spark in it. Before long she found herself getting into the swing of things. *This is one jumbie jamborée going on here.* And she began singing an old calypso song, her mother's favorite. *Back to back, belly to belly, I don't give a damn, I done dead already. Come on, nuh boys, punch it up, punch it up.* She danced the trays over the roller conveyor to their destination on the main line. She could feel the rattling from the trays traveling up her arms and the noise from the section behind her pummeling her bones as if she were one big conga drum vibrating in time to the bouncing trays and the piston rhythms. *Pshoop, number one piston in. Pshoop, number four piston in. Pshoop number three piston in. Oui foote. Back to back, belly to belly, in a jumbie jamboree.*

Since she had been at the plant, she had never seen such a commotion. It was as if all of them, that whole section, those shooting pistons, the torque checkers, the crank man, even she—it was as if all of them were loaded up with cow-itch, a stinging Trinidad plant, and had to dig deep into all parts of their bodies to relieve the itching. It seemed to her that they had scratched and scratched until they reached inside their souls and everything, everything was falling off of them: tiredness from the pistons, tiredness from the wiiirng wiiirng

wiiirng of the air guns, tiredness from someone always banging on the line and yelling *wake up muthafuckas.*

She wondered why the foreman was nowhere to be seen when the engine fell off the line but told herself *Better for us. Let him keep his tail wherever he is.* And she shuffled her feet and swung her big bottom right to left, *back to back, belly to belly,* shaking off the lonely days without her children and the ache for the sight of bright red anthuriums growing straight out of the ground and the salt breeze of Mayaro hitting her face. *I don't give a damn, I done dead already.*

No matter what ached in any of them, in her opinion, that morning was the most exciting in the history of Cadillac piston installation. It was the first time an engine had fallen off the line. When the two installers grabbed the engine back and front, said *heave ho,* and swung it onto its stand, the whole section broke out in raucous applause. The two responsible for replacing the engine bowed low and swept their arms to the floor as if they were courtiers. She bellowed *come on, boys, let us send this engine down the line in fine style,* and they all joined her for a chorus of jumbie jamboree. Their voices were so loud and strong they upped the speed of the line half a cycle. They didn't seem to care one bit because the renegade engine was headed out of their section on its way to the cam, timing chain, and front cover stations.

Come on, nuh boys, punch it up, punch it up. Let them all know we here and don't give a damn because we done dead already. She grabbed a piston from her checking tray and held it by both hands above her head, rocking it back and forth as if she were passing the review stand in the Savannah on opening day of Carnival, Port of Spain, Trinidad. *Oui foote. Let me hear the chorus. Back to back, belly to belly. We don't give a damn, we done dead already, we done dead already, we done dead already.*

Tuesday Morning

Buenas noches, mi Padrino.   ¿Como no quiere que llore?
Écheme la bendición.   ¿Como no voy a llorar?
Por adelante buena cara.   Una sola vida tengo
Por detrás me mordizcó.   y me la quiere quitar.

—TRINIDADIAN FOLK SONG

Her right hand emerged from the swaddle of blankets and waved languidly above her head, as if commanding every floorboard creak, wall shudder, and howl from the retreating Detroit night to be still. Then her hand passed over her exposed right cheek in a light ritualistic slap followed by a flurry of back-and-forth movements in front of her face, now cocked to the right, her head slightly lifted from the pillow. She flapped her hand inches from her nose and found nothing but chilled morning bedroom air. Aloneness quickly filled her as if sucked toward her body by some internal vacuum. Her right hand snaked back under the blankets as she lay there, eyes wide open, searching the thickness of the dark for something, anything that would assign meaning to her impending day world.

LOLITA HERNANDEZ

For some reason she saw her father at the bathroom sink, no, imagined him, in the same way she observed him preparing for work six mornings a week when she was a child. His image hovered in the front of her head, the place where all of her thoughts and dreams floated if she squeezed her eyes shut tight, which she did right then. She could move an image to the right or left, control the opening and closing of a mouth, replay a scene over and over until the emotion of it sank deep, deep somewhere in the back of her head. In this way, with her eyes closed, she heard inside of her the words of the song her father crooned every morning as he shaved to go to his job as a janitor. *¿Como no voy a llorar? ¿Como no voy a llorar?*

She drifted off to sleep without realizing that her cat, El Dorado, had not traipsed across her body two or three times, rubbed his entire length, head to upraised tail, across her face before his bewhiskered nuzzle in her ear. Get up. I'm hungry. He had set 4:45 each morning as his feeding time, fifteen minutes before her alarm rang during the work week. When El Dorado came calling for food, she would slap his whiskers away from her nose and turn her head away from his tuna breath. This morning she waved him away out of habit, even though he was not in the room.

As she slept she dreamed of a seagull sitting on a rock in the middle of an ocean, its shrill cries lost in the roar of the waves. The sea pounded and climbed the air around the gull but not a drop touched him. She was watching the gull, waiting for the moment their eyes could connect, when suddenly it flew toward a car full of her coworkers on a warm afternoon. They were by the river down the road from the plant. She couldn't hear a thing, even though their bodies moved this way and that and their mouths opened and closed. Big Mama sprawled across a car that could have been a Cadillac. More gulls came for bread; someone else not part of the group was throwing bread to the birds. She could see their hungry, evil faces as they swooped around the car. Big Mama waved her hand and they all disappeared.

At last the alarm rang, sending vibrations throughout the room. They traveled from the nightstand, disturbed the Boston fern hanging by the window, shook the art magazines on a footstool by the radiator. The feet of the nylon stockings hanging carelessly on the closet door danced. When the vibrations reached her body, her hand slipped from under the covers and located the first button on top of her nearly-new fuchsia-colored Magnavox radio/tape alarm. She stretched her body so that her fingertips touched the headboard and her toes reached for the foot of the queen-size bed and then contracted into a fetal position. Her back turned defiantly toward the clock; her arms locked between her legs. At that moment she could have easily masturbated, but that was too much effort. Her clitoris surged on its own. She locked her legs tighter and felt the pleasure. *How nice it would be to have a man here right now. Fuck the job. Fuck the world. I could lose myself under these covers with someone, anyone. Woooooahhhhh, shit.* Her body shivered. It was then that she missed the cat.

Sometimes a little thing like that can jolt your life and you wonder what it is that's different. All of a sudden, just like that, the cat isn't meowing for food before the alarm rings. Then the alarm goes off again and still no cat. *El Dorado, El Dorado.* She stretched her hand across to the right edge of the bed waiting for El Dorado's cold nose to explore her fingertips before he jumped up and began the food ritual. If he had done that, she would have stroked his long-haired, gray and white body, grabbed the top of his head with her hand, shaken it gently, and said, "Oh, El Dorado, I'll fix you up in just a few more minutes." But El Dorado didn't come and she drifted off wondering where he was and why she felt strange. She felt as if something horrible was looming. She tried to imagine the possibilities, but her mind was morning-foggy and she found herself drifting off while humming her father's song. It was the only thing she could focus on then and there. *Buenos noches mi Padrino. Una sola vida tengo y me la quiere quitar.*

She issued enough breath through her slightly parted lips to make a soft lullaby sound, but her jaws performed as if frozen; her lips barely moved. She couldn't distinguish if the melody floated in the room or in her head, but she knew that the words were out of order. At that moment her body seemed to rise up, float above itself. She felt as if she were everything and nothing. She was there and not there. Her skin peeled away and she was the room, the city, the world, a spirit free of the blankets and mattress. She lifted higher and higher outside of herself, inside of the world until she succumbed to the kind of heaviness she would feel after a night of drinking. After taking two aspirin to prevent the morning headache, she would sink the back of her head into the pillow, spread her arms across the bed, flex and tense her feet. Those times she slept in the middle of the bed. This is what happened that morning. She rolled to the middle of the bed and inside of her head she heard the voice of her father, in the moment when he would spread his arms to the mirror, shaving cream on his face, his merino vest wet from the morning ablutions, his sliders twisted on his portly waist. *Buenos días mi Padrino. Écheme bendición. Por adelante buena cara. Por detrás me mordizcó. Ah, yes. That was it.*

Then a procession of intake manifolds crossed her eyes. She was at her work station, near the beginning of motor line number two, where for three weeks she had been dropping manifolds onto the engine, a formidable task for her waifish body. The hoist was too high for her, the manifolds too heavy; she had to tiptoe to maneuver them. With each engine she inhaled and stole a glance at the people around her. She didn't want to appear weak.

Her father laughed at her the day she told him that she had made her ninety days at the plant. "Yes, you could have picked up the pen but, no, you picked up the hammer." "But Papa I picked up both." What did that mean? she now thought. It was a silly retort. The line drawings she completed, her failed attempt at art school, that wasn't the pen. Where was the dignity? Manifold after manifold looked like flying saucers flat and thick at the same time, a middle with ports, and mysterious passageways that channeled coolant around the firing chambers. She understood nothing about the metal. She understood nothing about the people.

Still there was no El Dorado in her bedroom to interrupt the procession of manifolds. By then he was parading himself on the kitchen counter, searching for a scrap of last night's dinner. El Dorado instinctively had learned to make do. He had adjusted to his mistress's new routine, which had begun to change gradually in the month or so since the old, loud, wind-up Big Ben quit working. Just like that. She had gone immediately after work that evening to Kmart and purchased something jazzy and reliable because, when she was late that morning, her foreman was all over her like white on rice, as they say in the factory. For the first few days she ignored El Dorado's nuzzling and waited for the alarm to ring before shifting her body on top of his and cuddling him. "Are you hungry, Eldy?" Then he would be fed. Soon she began responding to the alarm by pressing the snooze button. One snooze became two, two became three, and so on, like this morning.

It was becoming more difficult for her to get out of bed for work, but, like it or not, she needed the job. She hadn't figured out yet how to shuffle and grin her way through the work day or bitch and moan her way as so many others had. She was still intimidated by the complexity of the factory, all of the strange people, the noise. If she were there fifty years she could never accustom herself to the noise: a loud, white buzzing that traveled through her body, and commandeered it, pushing out every other thought in her head. She watched the woman working across from her, oblivious to everything. The man next to her was aware of everything, every bolt that fell, every bit of gossip. She had been there almost a year and hadn't found her niche. Maybe that was a sign there was no niche for her in that place. But she hadn't a notion of what else she could do or where she could go. There was comfort in the alarm ringing, her body rising to execute a predictable set of moves, walking out the door, walking in the plant up to her job, and surveying the manifolds before the buzzer rang. It sounded five minutes or so after her arrival. She believed in that much margin, no dashing in at the last minute for her. There was already enough tension in that place. This was why she pretended the buzz of the plant was the roar of the ocean. She had spent a day long ago at Big Sur listening to the waves crashing and watching a solitary seagull sit absolutely still on a jagged rock within swimming distance of the shore. He barely moved his head, and she sat just as still thinking of nothing. Not a thing. Salt water sprinkled her, and the motion of the waves, in and back out, calmed the rage inside of her.

Who knows why she was raging. She was at the tail end of adolescence and angry about everything: her brown skin, her good looks, her immigrant parents. She flopped this way and that in life, up and down, in and out of one thing or another. After the California trip, she returned to Detroit determined to please her parents, become responsible, and settle down. She enrolled in a few art courses at the university but she couldn't discipline herself enough to study. Her lifestyle was too spontaneous; she wasn't a self-starter. She grew tired of the gossip about her in the family and gravitated toward the factory, as a lark really, and for the good income. Her mother said, "Watch yuhself nuh, dahlin, in that place." Her father berated her. "*Sa çe couyont.*"

She should have awakened at the end of one snooze segment, nine minutes past 5:00 a.m. in order to arrive at work at least five minutes before 6:00 start-up. Instead she pushed the snooze again while figuring her next move. *Did I shower last night? Do I have to shower this morning?* She was still tired from the ten-hour shifts she had worked the previous two weeks. *Oh my god was I supposed to start at five this morning? What time is it?* She threw off the cover, swiveled her feet to the side of the bed, and grabbed its edge with her hands. Sweat beads formed on her forehead, her breathing became shallow and hot as she stared at the clock trying to figure out if she was already late for work. *What day is it?* Her mind engaged in a desperate chase of her body's activity the previous day, but she couldn't remember anything she had done. Did she go to work? Yes. Did she work the manifolds? Yes. What did she eat for lunch? Did she eat dinner last night? Did she shower last night? Ah, shower. Whenever she worked ten hours, she showered in the evening and went directly to bed. Otherwise, she preferred showering in the morning. She shuffled to the bathroom and saw that her towel was undisturbed. No shower last night. Ah, yes. The overtime ended last week. She was back to 6:00 a.m. shifts.

It was Tuesday and she was already two minutes into the second snooze segment. She crawled back into the bed, turned her face toward the clock, and lay there stiffly as she slowly pulled the covers over her body and up to her chin. She lay flat on her back waiting for the alarm to signal that she had better rush to the shower. She was, after all, running late by then, but she needed the extra time to sort herself out after all the excitement of not knowing if she was here or there, in yesterday or tomorrow. She tried again to fix herself in today. What is going to happen today? Anything special? No. *What should I wear? My new pink top? It's too pretty to wear on the line. But I need something today. I need something today.*

In this state she fell off to sleep and again found herself at Big Sur. The gull stood motionless in the midst of a storm, which buffeted her body, causing her to rock side to side. There was the gull on the rock island, calm, unruffled. She once asked her mother what it felt like to live on an island.

"Did you ever feel trapped on Trinidad with water all around you? You can only step so far in Trinidad and then there's the sea. You can't walk for days and days and days like you can here before you come to the end of land. I need to be able to walk for days and days, Mama, do you understand?" To which her mother replied, "You must learn how to swim, dahlin. You must learn how to swim."

So she moved from her spot on the shore and began to swim toward the gull on the rock but couldn't get past the first wave. She was sinking. Salt water filled her mouth and lungs. Her legs refused to move as she continued her descent.

When the alarm rang at 5:18, she opened her eyes and saw the rose-tinged grayness of dawn along the edge of the window blind. More than that she felt the pressure from her bladder and wanted to get up, go to the bathroom, begin the day, but she was still too tired. *My dreams are too restless.* If she lay in bed for one more snooze, by 5:27 her bladder would force her out of bed. She could shower quickly and arrive just in time for work. It's only seven minutes away in good traffic. It's late summer; the roads are fine; she doesn't always have to be on the job exactly five minutes before the bell rings and the line jerks forward. Come on let today be different. *Shit.* She trudged off to the bathroom in the dark and returned to her room in the dark, flopping herself across the bed. *El Dorado, El Dorado.* With several minutes still left before the alarm rang again, she sang to herself softly, *¿Como no voy a llorar? ¿Como no voy a llorar?*

Only the week before, she told her father, "You see, I named the cat El Dorado as a tribute to your country and to my job. You see how clever I am?" "*Pendeja*," he said. *Yes*, she said to herself as she lay across the bed. *Pendeja, pendeja.* She sang to the tune of Maria from *West Side Story*. *I've just met a girl named Pendeja. ¿Como no voy a llorar?* And she laughed.

Before long she was dreaming of the manifolds again. Now she was naked at her job. Her breasts tight and pointed, her flat bottom exposed to the main aisle, her curveless waist twisting to the right and back again to retrieve a manifold behind her and place it on a passing engine. Not a coworker commented on her nakedness. She worked hoping that she wasn't offending them in any way, but she had to teach them something. What? She worked as unself-consciously as possible, saying yes, this is the way we should all be. Finally, one of the men came up to her and said that at first he thought she was strange, "But it's O.K., it's O.K."

On the fourth ring of the alarm, she didn't open her eyes. She asked herself, *Why didn't I finish art school? I was right there. I was so close. Pendeja.* Queasiness arose in her stomach as she contemplated the biggest failure in her twenty-four years. *Por adelante buena cara. Por detrás me mordizcó.* Her hand sought the lower end of her torso in order to track the knot as it traveled from one side of her stomach to the other. Having pressed the snooze button, she fell asleep once again with her bowels feeling like wood and hot tears trickling down her cheeks.

El Dorado appeared in the doorway, content by then. He had eaten all of the dry cat food left in his tray and retrieved last night's Kentucky Fried Chicken bone from the garbage can. He moved noiselessly across the floor, jumped on the window ledge to check the traffic five floors below. He turned his attention to his mistress, who was flat on her back, snoring. He leapt onto the bed satisfied that she wouldn't be rising soon. Maybe it was Saturday. He barely had time to nestle into his favorite spot at the foot of the bed when the alarm rang again and her hand angrily slapped it quiet. El Dorado arose, arched his back, and left the room to seek his own peace on the couch.

There was still the slimmest chance that she could make it to work on time. It was 5:36 and still ticking. But she was on her stomach, splayed in a way that would require a great effort to move her extremities. They were far away from her brains. She dreamt of the gull, again. It was on its rock; it was by the section of the Detroit River close to the plant; it was in the plant riding a manifold. She was there also, naked. Everyone on the line was singing her father's song and he was serving them all coffee. Big Mama patted her on the back and said, "Heh, girlfriend, they've added more on my job."

She awoke, again the snooze. The alarm rang and was silenced several more times. Each time, in her dreams, she alternated scenes from her life as if trying to find the correct order. El Dorado came to the room once or twice to observe her movements, yawn, stretch, and leave.

Then she dreamt that she was sitting in her mother's kitchen, naked, asking her how it felt to be pregnant. "Like rolling down a long hill, gunga." Then they both were rolling down a hill laughing like schoolgirls. They were locked in each other's arms, their legs wrapped around each other. Her mother's glasses flew off, which made them both laugh uncontrollably. They began singing, "Matilda, Matilda, Matilda she take he money and run Venezuela."

The next ring of the alarm released a cawing cawing cawing in her room and she could hear wings flapping. It sounded like more than one bird. There were many gulls swooping and landing and flying around and swooping and cawing. She shot up in the bed, startled by the taste of the cold salt water as it splashed her face and dribbled into her mouth. Big waves washed over her but her body didn't move an inch. She said to herself, *I must be dreaming.* A wave passed over her, then the wind dried her off. Her body felt cooled by the wind and the water. Finally, she issued a loud, strong laugh and began to sing. At first the wind blew into her mouth, stealing the words of her song. *¿Como no voy a llorar? ¿Como no voy a llorar?* But the harder the wind blew, the louder she sang. *Una sola vida tengo y no me la puede quitar.*

Yes I Am a Virgin

There is a little mouse standing on its hind legs in the corner furthest from the door of the office where the lady is interviewing me. I can see its nose twitching and its front legs moving nervously. I think to myself, "Why don't you go away if you're so afraid?" But it just stands there sniffing the air, and I sit watching it, frozen because rodents have scared me ever since I was doing my homework in the kitchen of my parents' house when I was thirteen and all of a sudden I heard a crinkling noise and I couldn't figure out what it was and I looked up from a math problem and there were two teeny ears and a piece of a nose peering over the garbage pail in the kitchen by the sink. I ran screaming to my father because my mother was asleep. He said I was a fool. There was nothing to be afraid of. Then he smiled at me and said that he loved me. Then he said I had to continue what I was doing.

"Would you mind stating your name, job, and social security number for the record?"

She sounds like she belongs on one of those soap operas I never have time to watch because I'm either at work, or, when I'm at home, I'm running here and there doing something in the house or for the kids.

"I am Josie Morgan. Josephine Morgan. My number is 479-38-1372. I'm just an unskilled factory worker. I do whatever here."

"When was your first pregnancy?"

I never know if I'm seeing mice or baby rats. They used to tell me that the little critters scrambling around were baby rats but I don't know. It was the men telling me this. They'd yell out, Hey, Josie, there's a baby rat. And I'd yell back, How can you guys tell it's a rat? Looks like a mouse to me. What is the difference between a baby rat and a mouse?

"Did you receive a questionnaire in the mail about any negative experiences you may have had as a result of your pregnancy during your employment at General Motors?"

"I think so, Miss. I'm not sure. I don't always read my mail. Sometimes the kids get to it. Sometimes I don't care. Bill collectors. You know. Junk mail." From a distance they look the same, I guess. I don't even know. Back then they just told me I was looking at baby rats. Maybe I was looking at mice and they were fooling me.

"Do you know why we are questioning you?"

I wonder if that is a mouse or baby rat in this office now.

"We are here today because we want to make sure that someone like you has not been missed in the mailing."

I was the only woman out of ten press operators on the hood reinforcement line on afternoons when I started. So they could have been ribbing me a lot. I didn't bother to tell anybody that I was scared to death of mice and rats.

"We are asking all of the women who hired in before December 1973 whether or not they felt they were discriminated against while they were pregnant as a General Motors employee. Do you understand that?"

Then again, some people call mice rats because it's all the same to them. There is a difference to me even though I am afraid of them both equally. One grows big and one stays little. So seems like I'd be more afraid of rats because they get bigger, especially in the factory. But I am afraid of mice as much as rats because they can sneak up on me.

"Have you received in the mail any literature about the UAW class action suit regarding the issue of pregnancy in the plant prior to 1973?"

"Oh no. I was already frightened by them. The factory didn't do that. The mice and rats are just here. I always ask myself, If you are so afraid of mice, why do you stay here all this time?"

"What are you talking about?"

"My Jimmy is seven and Mary is five but she's fast as a whip. She's really five going on forty-five."

"And did you have any problems doing your job during your pregnancies?"

"I did o.k. with Jimmy, but with Mary I had trouble. Just like a girl, especially that one—she was inside me raising hell. I mean, I was able to stay on the job until the top of the ninth month with Jimmy."

"What kind of work do you do?"

"I've been doing about the same kind of job ever since I hired in here. I'm a press operator on the hood reinforcement line. When I get the Cadillac hood, it's just sheet metal. Me and whoever my partner is grab the metal, lay it on the press. Then I press my buttons, my partner presses his, and boom you got a hood. Kind of. Next stop on our line some other stuff gets done and so on until there's a finished hood."

"You worked that press until your ninth month?" This is the first time she looks up at me.

"I'd like to ask you . . ."

"Well did you feel that management at any time made things difficult for you? Did management make you take time off that you didn't want?"

"Miss, what is your name?" She looks down again.

"Did you lose wages because of management harassing you during your pregnancy?"

"Who do you work for, Miss?"

"Julia Worthingham. I work for Cadillac Labor Relations."

"Are you afraid of mice?"

"Mice? No. Mice? I never see them. I don't know. I don't guess so."

"You work for the company?"

"In a way yes. I'm an intern in Cadillac Labor Relations. Actually, I'm a student at Detroit College of Law specializing in labor relations."

She smiles at me a little this time. All of a sudden I feel real stupid.

"As part of my job, I am questioning Cadillac women who may have suffered discrimination because of their pregnancy while working for Cadillac Motor Car Company."

She doesn't want to hear all that stuff about my girl. All she wants is the facts. Like we are in court or something.

"Can we get back to the interview? When was your first pregnancy? Let me rephrase that. How many pregnancies have you had?"

Just then Rex comes bopping past the foreman's cubicle where Miss Worthingham is quizzing me. He starts making funny faces at me in the window behind her back. He sort of hikes up his chest, throws his head back, and struts up and down in front of the office—his way of saying that Miss Worthingham looks stiff.

What a name, Worthingham.

"So you had no problems whatsoever with management during your pregnancies?"

I wonder if Worthingham ever had any kids. I wonder if she ever did any more work than study at school and go around asking people their business.

"Well I guess that concludes the interview."

No, not yet. "My foreman during both my pregnancies was Pete. He was sweet as he could be. One of the few decent foremen around here. He bent over backwards to help me out, though, like I said, with the second one—nobody could really help me. Nature had to take its course—nature and the good Lord."

Miss Worthingham looks at me for a quick minute and sort of scrunches up her eyebrows. I start to feel uneasy about Rex jumping up and down outside the office. Rex stands at the office window looking in. I motion for him to go away. He just stands there. Then Big George comes sauntering by and stares in the window. Then Marianne, Louis, Bertha, Max. Here they come one right after another peeping in. I get a big smile on my face. The mouse or rat is standing straight up in a corner behind Miss Worthingham. I want to laugh, but I don't.

"Go ahead, Josephine. When was your first pregnancy?"

"Oh yeah, no problem with the first, but like I said I had trouble with Mary and had to go out on a medical. I had those fibroid tumors come up and I kept being in pain, and the doctor said I could miscarry. The first time it happened I was in my third month and had to stay off work nearly two months.

Then when I went back to work, the pain came up again and I had to go off until I had the baby. Funny thing is, I haven't been bothered by those tumors since."

"Specifically what kind of job do you do here? Actually, what kind of work were you doing at the time of your pregnancies?"

"I did whatever. Things were looser on afternoons when the brass went home and left the plant in charge of the foot soldiers." Miss Worthingham was starting to squirm in her chair. "There was rhythm on the hood line—foomp da da, foomp da da. All together foomp da da."

"Josephine, for the record, when were your children born?"

"Two, only two."

"Could you give me exact birth dates?"

"It's funny how things come back to me all of a sudden. You're here asking me about how it is being pregnant in the plant, and it takes me all the way back to my first day, September 6, 1968."

"Very well, thank you Miss ahhhh . . ."

"Morgan. Just call me Josie. I was fresh out of high school. I couldn't think of what else to do. It's not that I didn't do o.k. in school. I took college prep courses but by the time graduation day rolled around, I was tired of studying. I thought I'd go out and make some money for myself, have a good time for a while, then see about hitting the books. I guess I got here and got stuck."

"You started working here when you were eighteen?"

She scared it away when she raised her voice. It went right in between that crack over yonder. It must have been a mouse and not a rat because I heard that rats aren't limber enough to squeeze through cracks like that critter just did.

"You will receive a document in the mail within a week summarizing what we have talked about today."

I don't want her to stop the interview so soon, and to have to go back to the job. I don't want her to be afraid of the clank, clank of the presses and the oil and dirt and stuff. She must see something in my face, because she twirls her head around so fast I hear her neck bones crack like an old man's. Then she says, "Who are they? What are they doing?"

"It's break time." She is starting to look a little nervous. "Please take the time to read the document when you receive it in the mail. Does the plant have your correct address?"

"Oh, Miss Worthingham, this is Connor Stamping, the home of the Cadillac clowns. We have the wildest, craziest people in all of Cadillac working over here. I think it's because of the noise from the presses and it's so dark and grimy in here. They don't mean nothing. They're my good friends just having a little fun with me."

"Very well. Thank you, Miss ahh . . ."

She couldn't have ever had any kids. Her body is too slim. Well maybe she had one and has a maid or a good husband so she can work out at the gym two-three times a week. Maybe even four times. Can you have a husband and go to school? Who knows with women like her? Anyone with hair that blond and shiny can't be doing a whole lot of work.

"If you have had no problem with management during your pregnancies . . ."

I sort of linger for a minute remembering things. I must have a remembering look on my face because she asks me if anything is wrong.

"Yes, Miss." She looks at me for a minute then straightens out some papers. Maybe she is stiff. Really, the only thing that saves her from looking mean is her blond hair all floofed up around her face.

"You can go now. Please tell the foreman to send in Sue James. Thank you."

Yeah, the interview office is just like Greene's was. Same two-drawer file cabinet and gray steel desk with a piece of plastic covering notes, a bookcase type of thing with some manuals on top, a gray wastebasket, a phone, and a plug-in radio. Nothing fancy, except the office I am in with Miss Worthingham is beginning to take on some of her perfume smell. "What's the name of the perfume you're wearing, Miss?"

"L'Interdit by Givenchy."

Foreman Greene's office smelled like cigar smoke and farts. Greene and a couple of other foremen used to hang out there during most of the shift with a couple of janitors.

"Do you remember something else?"

"The foreman I had when I hired in called me in for a talk a few days after I started. His office was just like this one, dirty and cramped."

"Is this the foreman you have now?"

"No, he's not my foreman anymore."

"O.K., Josie, have your current foreman send the next person in."

"I haven't been in a foreman's office in a long time since then. I try to avoid it. That's why I don't come in late or leave early or get into any kind of trouble because I don't like a foreman's office."

"Do you remember any trouble?"

"I saw my first rat in the plant when I walked down the aisle to his office. No mistaking it. Huge, big as a cat."

Miss Worthingham looked at me over her glasses.

"Don't let anybody fool you; factory rats are so fat they're sassy. People around here leave food for them just like they're pets. If somebody drops some food on the floor or something, they just leave it for the rats. We got cats around here, too, but they're not up to handling the rats. Too skinny, can't get to the food."

"Did they frighten you with rats when you were pregnant?"

"No, ma'am, I was already afraid of them." She works for the company. No wonder we are having this interview inside the plant. I thought if she were with the UAW we would meet at the Local or some place away from the plant.

LOLITA HERNANDEZ

56

"We are here today because we want to make sure that someone like you has not been missed."

"Thank you, Miss. My name is Josephine. Are you afraid of mice or baby rats? Or big rats?"

"Rats? No. Rats? I never see them. I don't know. I don't guess so."

"You know, I looked good like you when I hired in. My hair was nice and shiny blond like yours. I had a figure."

"Can we get back to the interview?"

Just then Greene, the foreman, comes by the office. He looks through the window behind her back and makes a funny face at me. He puts his hands by his chest and moves them up and down like he had boobs there. Then he throws his head back and laughs. Miss Worthingham looks at me for a long time. "Josie, is there any chance I might run across one of those rats today?"

"I'm so careful about where I walk in here," I say to myself, "that I take the same path every day to let the rats know they should walk someplace else and stay out of my way."

"I work for Cadillac Labor Relations. Maybe we can get the plant cleaned up."

I have to laugh. "Miss, you've probably run across a dozen or so two-legged rats already in this place. Especially good looking as you are."

"What?" That's all Miss Worthingham says. Her mouth hangs open and she is on the edge of her chair.

"You see, Miss, Bill Greene called me into the office, I thought to give me some kind of orientation or job instructions. He had me sit in a chair, looked me up and down and asked me if I was a virgin."

"What?"

"Yeah, he asked me if I was a virgin."

"What did you do? What did you say?"

"I told my mother. She said to pray. I went to church that Sunday and prayed. I'm Catholic, you know."

"What happened then? What did he do? What did he say?"

"Bill Greene called me into the office two-three more times. I was so young then. The last time he called me in the office, which was about my second week in the plant, I just blurted out, Yes, yes I am a virgin. So what? It's none of your business anyway. He said for me to go do whatever. He said that I was a fool. I ran out of the office. I caught a glimpse of him over my shoulder laughing at me."

"Did you tell anyone what happened? Did you tell his boss?"

"By break time that night damn near everybody in the place was calling me a virgin."

"Look, I'm just an intern from Detroit College of Law."

"Maybe because I'm a white girl and I got along so well with the black guys, he was testing me or something."

"Did you have any problems specifically while you were pregnant?"

"I've been doing about the same kind of job ever since I hired in here. Like I told you, I'm a press operator on the hood reinforcement line. When I get the Cadillac hood, it's just sheet metal. Me and whoever my partner is grab the metal, lay it on the press. I press my buttons and my partner presses his. The die goes down and there's the hood. Kind of. Next stop on our line some other stuff is done and so on until there is a finished hood. There's rhythm to our line. Foomp da da, foomp da da."

"You will receive a document in the mail summarizing what we have discussed about your pregnancies."

"After that everybody wanted to know who my boyfriend was, who I was fucking. It was embarrassing having my business out in the street. Things died down for a while until I got pregnant, then there it was again. Folks were saying, Guess you're not a virgin now."

"Please sign the document."

"Of course you're new here and still so young. Being a lawyer and all, how folks treat you around here might make a difference to you."

"I assume the plant has your correct address. Return the document in the envelope provided."

"But for me, now that I've had a couple of kids and a couple of bad husbands to boot, I just take everything in stride. The men in here hardly mess with me anymore. I guess they figure I'm no day at the beach so why bother?"

"Please ask your foreman to send in Susan James."

"Oh, they might tease me about my weight or tell me I can't keep a man or offer me a few bucks in trade now and then, especially after they've been drinking. One time they put a dead rat in a box and gave it to me at Christmas. But I just do whatever I have to do to make it in life and everything else rolls right off my back."

Float

She was letting her mind float again. This time she was being a rock, sitting still still still on a railing in a second-floor corner of the plant with her broom lying up against her. No one ever told her how to be a rock. That she had to discover for herself. After sitting for who knows how long, she felt her skin for hardening. Had she become a smooth rock or one with ridges and rough edges with bits of black dirt embedded in it? Had a fossil formed on her too? But she couldn't feel the outside of herself just then because, of course, a rock had to be still; a rock couldn't move to touch itself.

So then she concentrated on the inside of a rock. What does the inside of a rock feel like? Come to think of it, at first when she was trying to be a rock, she was trying to be the outside of the rock. Now then, she said to herself, I will try to be the inside of the rock and I will be able to feel myself without having to move.

Then she thought and thought about the inside of a rock and realized that it must move; there must be running hot streams inside of a rock or else why would the outside have to be so hard? Yes, that was it. The outside was so hard in order to keep the running hot liquid inside or else it would scorch everyone and everything that it ever came into contact with.

What if she seeped out of one of the cracks in the rock's surface? A rock can have cracks in it. She remembers having seen at least one like that. She felt her insides swell and retreat, swell and retreat. So there, she told herself, maybe this rock doesn't have a crack in it. Again she could feel her insides swell and retreat in its search for an escape.

All of a sudden she felt a trickle of heat run down her left arm. It dribbled until it reached the second finger of her left hand, and it felt good to her to have some of the liquid come out. Then she remembered what her mother used to say to her a long time ago: You have a head as hard as a rock. You're not like the others. Sometimes I wish you were never born. Her mother used to tell her that. So she got it into her head that she was a rock, not like everyone else. She really did want to be like the others.

The liquid began trickling down her arm until it reached the second finger of her left hand, when it settled into the biggest drop of liquid she had ever seen remain a drop before it burst out of itself and then run off somewhere. So this big bubble of liquid that had just escaped from the crack in her rock-skin lingered on the edge of her fingertip. She watched it out of the corner of her eyes. She watched and watched until the bubble of liquid burst and was ready to drip from her fingertip. Well if she didn't do something quickly that bit of liquid that had just previously found its way out through a crack in her surface would end up on the floor. She didn't want that to happen, a bit of her insides on the floor. She had worked too hard to find her insides and get them out only to have them spill on the floor.

So she raised her finger to allow the liquid to flatten out, cling to her finger, then roll down the underside of her left arm. If she leaned her whole body to the right the liquid could find its way back inside of her. She figured the liquid probably came out through a valve in her heart. She lifted her left arm way up high with the middle finger extended and leaned to her right. She sat very still like that for who knows how long, and she could feel the stuff from inside of her finding its way back in. She realized that the liquid seeping back in did not have the same power as it had when seeping out because it didn't have the swell and retreat of all of the liquid inside of her to help push it back in the way it had been pushed out. She realized that maybe she had to move ever so gently to allow the liquid to find the crack it came out of and ease back into her.

That was how her foreman found her, sitting on a railing in a second-floor corner with her hand up in the air gyrating slowly, the way you move a handheld, miniature pinball game, the game where you try to put five, six, or seven little balls in their respective holes. That's how the foreman found her. He called plant security right away and then her committeeman and they all escorted her out of the building. The committeeman applied for a medical leave on her behalf and she was out of the plant until months later.

The next time she was in the ladies' bathroom on the first floor. That's where they assigned her to work. She was still a janitor, but had been reassigned to a different area and a different foreman. They thought maybe the change would help her. It was after the time that mostly everyone had already had their breaks so she was pretty much alone again. Things usually happened when she was alone and there was no one around to distract her. She really didn't like to talk to people too much anyway because all they ever wanted to talk about was jive nonsense. That's what she was thinking when she started to put the disinfectant in the toilet bowls so she could swab them out. Jive nonsense. She put disinfectant in the bowls just as they had taught her. She squirted it under the rim around and around and let it sit for a few minutes. She had numbered the toilets so she wouldn't get confused; there were six in all. So she started at number one, squirt and swirl, squirt and swirl, until she reached number six, squirt and swirl, squirt and swirl. Then she went back to number one, swabbed round and round, swabbed round and round, until she reached number six toilet. Then she returned to number one, flush away, flush away, fast fast. She quickly went to number two, then three, until she reached number six again. Then she rushed back to number one and repeated the flushing sequence. She liked the swirling splashing noise the toilets made just after the plunging sound. And she liked the sucking sound at the end of the flushing; it was very similar to when she was a child and she had straws to suck lemonade and she would get to the end of the glass of lemonade and suck suck suck the air around the remaining ice.

Also she liked to get all of the toilets swirling at once because she could close her eyes and pretend she was at the ocean. She had never been to the ocean because she came from a little town in Ohio that didn't have much water in it, but she had seen shows about the ocean on television and she knew how the ocean sounded all right. Whoooosh whooosh whooosh.

That was how a lady who worked on the motor line found her when she entered the restroom. She was dancing from one toilet to another flushing them and going whooosh whooosh whooosh. She had the swabbing brush in her hand and the lady was afraid that she would want to use it on her. That's easy enough to understand. So she ran out quickly and told the foreman who called plant security and the committeeman and they all came running and all those men went into the ladies' room where they saw her dancing from toilet to toilet. Immediately they escorted her from the plant. The committeeman fixed up her papers and she went out on another medical for a long time.

When she returned to the plant they put her to work in salvage. One of the reasons was because she would have the same committeeman and would be in the same supervisory pool so that everyone would be familiar with her, you know, in case. She worked like the devil in salvage, stuffing the giant compactor with trash. She was just like the others picking through the trash. She found all sorts of interesting things like old tubes of lipstick, an empty whiskey bottle, a bible. You name it. Some of what she found she put in her locker. You can never tell when these might come in handy, she thought.

She was very good at compacting trash. She worked at that job until the spring came and then the summer. She began to sit outside in the courtyard between the final drive department and salvage, like everyone else. She sat on a concrete ledge and drank juice at break time and ate her lunch that she bought from the cafeteria every day. Then it occurred to her that she couldn't see any trees from where she sat in the salvage court-yard. So she started eating her lunch across the street while sitting on the railing outside of the medical department directly across from the courtyard. That was o.k. at lunchtime; she could see the trees because they would let her sit outside of the salvage area then. But when she was on her break she couldn't see the trees because they didn't let anyone leave the area just to cross the street. She would still be on Cadillac property but the security guards back then weren't very nice. They would stop you from doing the simplest things like going to the yuck truck one or two minutes before your official lunch even if the truck was sitting right outside the plant door.

It bothered her that there were no trees inside of the courtyard where everyone took their midmorning or midafternoon breaks. So she thought about how she had been such a successful rock and she figured that if she concentrated really hard on all of the elements of a tree she could be a tree for the salvage courtyard. It would also take her mind off of feeling trapped in the plant.

She sat and thought for a long time about being a tree. She didn't waste any time thinking about the outside of a tree. She already knew that if she thought about the inside of the tree she would automatically become the outside of it, brown and rough on the bottom with lovely green fluttering leaves on the top like the little trees she used to draw when she was a little girl at school. She would bring them home to her mother who wouldn't even look at them at first, but then she kept saying, Mama look, Mama look, and her mother would look and say that's nice. She couldn't blame her mother for not being excited because she was tired all the time. There were five children in her family and no father to bring home money. He left one day just like that. When he left, her mother cried a whole lot, then she got angry, then she started doing people's laundry until she got a job taking care of other people's children.

Basically she had good memories about trees, which was why she wanted trees in the salvage courtyard. So she thought and thought how stringy the inside of a tree must be. She liked that part because when she was drawing trees as a child she could never draw the inside and somehow her trees always felt a little incomplete.

Now she would become a complete tree. She sat very still on her break one day on the ledge over by the final drive area with both of her arms lifted high up to the sky. The day was so sunny that even the courtyard was bright. As soon as she felt stringy and full of veins and sappy like the inside of a tree her arms started to wave back and forth with the gentle breeze passing through the courtyard. Soon a little woo woo woo sound escaped from her lips as the breeze whistled through her branches.

That was how they found her, after everyone else had reported back to work. Her coworkers had seen her outside but they thought that she would return to work after the break. When the foreman didn't see her at her station stuffing the compactor, he asked everyone where she was. A jitney driver said, I think she is outside praying. Another driver said, no she is outside stretching. One of the people who worked directly with her said, she is outside being a tree. They all laughed, except the one who said she was being a tree. We shouldn't laugh at her, he said.

The foreman said, oh shit and went out to investigate. Sure enough he found her out there, the breeze whistling in her branches. He called security and her committeeman and said, we have to do something. She is being a tree. It had been a bad day for the foreman all around: the compactor was acting up; he was short two jitney drivers to haul the trash bins to salvage, and now she was being a tree.

There she was again going on another medical. They fixed up her papers and let her stay off for a while until she stopped being a tree.

When she returned they told her maybe you should sling some steel, do something that would keep you busy all the time. So they put her in the plating department lifting bumpers, because she was a big woman and not so old that she couldn't do heavy work. Nobody worried about her having children; so what difference did it make if she did heavy work? Besides she did a fine job there for a long time, until one day a cat wandered into the department. It was a scrawny little black thing that followed everyone down the aisles and all around. It followed the ladies into the restroom. It even followed her. Actually the cat took a liking to her and would sit with her at break time and at lunchtime, and in the afternoon it would nap in her lap. Oh how she loved having that little furry cat in her lap. Everyone fed the cat; it eventually became fat and sassy. She brought it cans of tuna. The cat had long hair. In fact she got a kick out of the fact that the cat's hair was longer than hers. Sometimes she put the cat on top of her head and pretended it was a wig. The cat didn't mind; it purred and purred.

One day the cat had kittens, two little fuzzy balls someone found one morning in the cat's sleeping box. No one had realized the cat was pregnant. They just thought that she was getting fat because of the food they were feeding her, and also her hair was so long it was hard to tell. Also she only carried two kittens, which were so tiny that there hadn't been enough of them to make her sides poke out.

When the kittens were six weeks old, a man took one and a lady took another and then someone else took the mama to the vet to be fixed and never brought her back. That was it for her friend. No more cat. She missed that cat so much. Lunch didn't seem the same; breaks didn't seem the same. She thought and thought about that cat until they found her slinking around the corners one day on all fours. She sounded like a motor because, of course, she was content and purring her heart out. She started meowing and rubbing up against everyone's legs, even the women's. She pissed in the corner where the other cat had had its litter box. That was it. The foreman called the committeeman and the two of them called security and this time they figured there was no hope for her. They were going to try to put her out of the plant on a permanent medical.

When security came to escort her out she hissed and scratched and carried on something fierce. No one had seen a battle like that in a long time at that plant. Then they called a couple of more security guards; even the committeeman, a small wiry man, had to help hold her in order to get her out. One of the ladies working nearby said, please be careful; she is a woman. Then the lady got into the act trying to calm her down. That worked and they were able to get her out of the plant, which is where she still is now.

Preparing for a Strike

🐦

"It was a summer of fires and shark attacks."
—DAVID BROOKS, from "Blue"

"She is gorgeous and knows it,
 and always wants to cut my hair short
 and style it up high like hers.
 I almost always agree,
 because who wouldn't want to look like her"
—AMY DRYANSKY, from "Permanent"

The feeling had been building in us ever since we asked one of the guys with thirty-five years seniority, "Hey, how do you think it's going to go with the strike?" And he said, "I don't know. It could go any kind of way. This is a strange one this year. I can't get a fix on it."

Now the guy who was telling us this has seen lots of strikes in his day. So for him not to have a fix on this strike was a bad, bad sign, and caught us off guard. We're used to steady work. Most of us have never seen a strike or even a layoff, even when we had that spontaneous work stoppage a while back after the foreman fired one of the guys for being late. We all knew that everything would work out fine. We were just flexing our muscles a little because the foreman was flexing his. We knew he didn't really mean to fire anybody.

This strike was shaping up to be more than muscle-flexing. Too many complicated issues that none of us understood. We weren't sure that the union guy understood the issues either, but every drop of sweat on his forehead spelled trouble when he waddled onto the floor with a checklist of people in his district. He's just a small potato in a big sack. Still, we felt sorry for him having to do all that walking in the district because he is short and fat and breathes heavily when he has to be on the floor, which is rarely, because of the shortness of breath problem, especially in the heat. Usually he walks the main aisles or the outer side of the line. That way he can call across to someone on the other side or pass a flyer without hoisting his big belly over the moving line.

This time he crossed and recrossed the line, squeezed and grunted between boxes of stock and equipment in order to get to folks on break in corners or hidden by massive machines. He gave every single person a piece of paper with the names of strike team members. Each list had a star by the name of the strike captain. None of us knew how the captains were chosen. We were so happy to see the union man and at least find out about the teams that it didn't make a difference.

We slapped him on the back good-naturedly and wished him well because long before the union man came around we had begun making our own plans. For weeks we discussed things amongst ourselves, studied every line on the face of every foreman who spoke to any of us about anything. We gauged their walk, cocky and confident, or stooped and demoralized. Those of us who had contacts with higher level managers made it our business to stay close to them in order to read between the lines about the health of the facility or to find out if any of our jobs had been shipped out, making us replaceable. Those who were tight with various levels of union representatives stuck with them, pumping them gently for information that might help us construct a picture of the strike.

Like I said, the confirming blow was when we asked the man with thirty-five years what he thought, and he gave us double-talk. That told us what we needed to know about the strike: how long, how intense, and so on. Vital information for our lives, mostly how we should save our money, what we should tell our families. It was clear to us, without any of us ever actually saying it, that the strike would be so long and so intense it could cost us our jobs.

So we started making lists. One of the guys had seen a coupon ad for simonizing cars over at a place on the west side. Real cheap and quite a few of the guys had had cars done there before, and the place did good work. Real good work. So the guy who had seen the ad in the newspaper started clipping the coupons and giving them out. I think the coupons were in the paper every Thursday. He told a few others and pretty soon the whole shop was clipping the coupons for those who maybe didn't get the paper and also friends of ours who didn't even work in the shop. So the first list was of all the people who didn't have a simonize coupon so we could make sure they had one. I was thankful one of the guys put my name on the list because, as usual, the ship was getting ready to leave the dock without me, and I wasn't even packed. Which is to say that I wasn't even aware of the coupon. But the guys took care of me. Thank goodness, too, because Lord knows every little bit helps.

Next one of the ladies announced that she had found a place where you could get insulated windows installed real dirt cheap, and she had several friends who already had them in their houses over the last winter and their heating bills fell by this incredible amount. Of course, everybody swooped in on that one (except me because I rent). I helped make up a list anyway just so I could do my part. When you're getting ready for a strike, you can't be selfish and say you don't want to do such and such because it doesn't directly pertain to you. In a strike situation it really is one for all and all for one.

Of course, the guy who works right next to me would be the one to remember that dental coverage is the first to go when a job ends, and we were all sure that we would lose our jobs. He always has some medical problem or another in his family. His wife was in a car accident not long ago. She was cracked up pretty bad. I'm glad that happened then and not now. He said the same thing. His kids are always breaking something or other because they play sports in school. That poor man. I don't know how he's going to make out. Plus his asthma.

Because of him we all got on the case with the dentist. Every dentist in the area was flooded with our appointments. I have three children so you know I called for an appointment. It was the least we could do: go out with clean healthy teeth and hope that something comes up soon so we could get dental coverage again. We didn't exactly make a list for dental appointments, but he took it upon himself personally to go around every day and check that people made their appointments and that they kept them.

The biggest list, surprisingly, was the one for Italian tiles. One of the guys had a connect with someone who could get him the tiles directly from Italy. He fixed his kitchen up with them in case he had to sell his house, because the value would go up. That's what he told us. He had the whole process down pat. One day he gave us a lecture on how to lay those tiles. In order to cut them, you have to score them, and then they crack. Something like that. He brought in a couple of tiles to show us, the ones he put on the floor and the ones he put along the edge of his kitchen wall to about waist high. All of the tiles were blue and brown with florets and fancy lines along the edges. The floor tiles were brown with blue florets; the wall tiles were the opposite, blue with brown florets. He lined them up along one of the benches at right angles and you could see how the combination would look great.

The guys got pretty emotional about the whole thing. They ordered tiles for their wives as a last something ritzy they could give them before the money ran out. Two of the guys ordered the same brown and blue combination. Others ordered salmon and blue, green and blue, white with gray accents, and a kind of exotic aqua with peachy florets. It was all very tender. I listened to so many of them tell me how much they loved their wives and so on. You could see a few eyes glazing over like they wanted to cry. One did, behind the block washer. Between sobs he said, "I know a man is not sup-posed to cry." I said, "Oh, honey, it makes you more of a man if you can," and I gave him a big hug.

It was like death approaching or something. Geez it was spooky, but I listened because I knew it was part of everyone being really uptight about the strike and knowing we might never return to the job. That's the way things are these days: you go out on strike and never get back in and then you're scuffling around in some nickel-and-dime job because your good job has gone down the tubes. So you have to stand up and fight about certain issues otherwise the company will stick it to you so bad that the good job ends up not being worth anything anyway. We all knew that: better to die with dignity than crawl around like worms for the rest of our lives. That's what we kept trying to tell ourselves, not knowing if solidarity forever could really work in our case. The world is so different since UAW organizing drives like the Battle of the Overpass or the Flint sit-down strikes. We felt so helpless.

So, I listened to them and they listened to me. I don't like to complain or publicize my problems; it always makes you seem so weak, being a woman and all. I mean a man can whine on and on about his problems (and they always do, don't fool yourself), but let a woman utter one sad word, and they'll start talking about how weak she is. So I tend to put up this front; a lot of women I work with do.

I didn't tell the guys about how really scared I was of losing the job. I didn't tell them I didn't have a man to help me when things get tough, or even another set of shoulders to cry on. You can't really cry to your kids. Although my father once said when he was living (God rest his soul) that it is good for kids to see their mothers cry to let them know what they go through. Still I hate to let my kids see me cry because they get scared, and then I feel even worse. So I told the guys about how handy I am with needle and thread, about how I sew almost all my kids' dress-up clothes (which is true). I told them that I knew I could start up a little business. Plus I'm handy with craft things, making fancy baskets, silk floral arrangements, doodads to hang on the refrigerator, specialized mailboxes. I can build the wood parts and decorate them, lettering and all. I could get a stall at the flea market and move into a shop when things got going good.

I didn't want any Italian tiles, because like I said, I rent, and you don't need Italian tiles with three kids all under ten. But I found a coupon for "a day of delight" at a beauty shop not far from work. That's what they called it, "a day of delight at Kara's House of Esquisite Beauté." You could get the complete works at a discount: facial, pedicure, manicure (the kind where they massage your hands), body massage, new hairdo. The way the coupon was set up, before you entered the shop you could mark off what you wanted to have done if you didn't want the entire package. I guess that's so you don't go in there and get overwhelmed and waste their time hemming and hawing. Someone like me would do that because my nails never get manicured, the girl next door cuts my hair, and I cut hers, and the only massage I get is when my littlest one walks on my back when I fall asleep on the floor in front of the TV. Also, I avoid open-toed shoes in the summer.

The funniest thing about the coupon: I didn't share it with anyone. I didn't tell a soul about it. Not that the guys themselves could use it, but it could have been one of those things they gave their wives for the last. You know what I mean? I studied that coupon all by myself at home where no one could peek over my shoulder and say, "Hey, what's that?" I made my appointment pretty close to strike deadline so I could go out in style. I made my selection for the whole enchilada, everything. I wanted the complete, no-holds-barred beauty treatment.

I walked into the beauty shop the morning of the appointment, and I was just getting ready to show the lady my coupon, when in walks one of the ladies from work. There aren't too many of us working in our department. We kind of giggled at each other. Neither one of us said anything goofy like, "Do you come here often?" or "Fancy meeting you here." I knew and she knew we were making special preparations. How could you talk about that to anyone? How could you say you wanted a facial that would remove years of blackheads and close your pores? How could you say that what was most important was getting nails so slick and pretty you could start running your fingers through your beautiful new hairdo and not feel embarrassed? You might even stop biting your nails. Here you were on a hot summer morning in a salon that would massage away every single year you spent in that dump making enough money to pay the car note so you would have something to drive to work the following week. Of course, now there might not be a following week, but you'll be cute.

I rolled up the section of newspaper I had in my hand with the full-page "a day of delight coupon" in it and thwacked her on the thigh. She sank down in a chair next to mine where we began waiting for our turn. She giggled some more, rolled her big green eyes at me, and shifted her top lip as far right as possible, her lower lip as far left as possible. Then one eye closed, the other squinted and stared straight ahead like some kind of Halloween creature. "After they're through with you in here you won't be making crazy faces like that," I said.

"Let's go for a beer afterwards, kiddo," she said.

"You got it, babe."

Then the receptionist motioned for me to go to the changing room. "The massage is first. Strip to your panties and put on one of those powder blue gowns," she said. For a minute I thought I was going for my annual GYN exam. I decided to view my body in the mirror that spanned the double sink. Not bad, I told myself. A few stretch marks, a little bit of a roll, but passable, real passable. I'm not so bad as a woman, but of course I was in a loose mood at the House of Beauté, looking forward to a new me. So I was in the frame of mind to reevaluate myself, make a sow's ear into a silk purse. Then I saw the sign on the upper left corner of the mirror: Unisex.

That's all I needed. Some man barging in on me while I was staring at my chest. I double-checked the lock on the main door because the changing room was set up so that the toilet stall had its own separate lock. Anyone could walk into the main changing room area. I wasn't exactly ready for sharing this body.

This story is not about a man barging in on me in the changing room. It's about how naked I felt while looking at myself in the mirror. Oh, I hate guilt. I was standing in the mirror of the changing room, remembering all of the sins I had committed against the company: the times I took too long for break, snuck out early, snuck in late. I would feel then as if I were unclothed in the middle of the main aisle of my department, everyone looking at me. That naked. Hundreds of eyes crawling over every inch of my body. Feasting on my nipples, looking to see if my ass sagged, checking for stretch marks.

Looking in that mirror I couldn't get over being in the House of Beauté, my car simonized the day before, dental appointments for the following day, and not one of the guys, not one knew about the coupon. On Monday morning, they will know, I told myself. My blackheads will be gone. My hair flipped up a new way. I'll have on makeup to match my new hairdo. More than likely I'll be walking straight as an arrow after the massage.

Still I'll have that old guilty naked feeling. What should I do? Cover my eyes so I won't see them seeing me? Or pretend I'm not naked? I could make a list of all kinds of smart responses like, "Hey guy, you could spend a year in a beauty shop and come out with the same case of uglies." I could practice how to flip my new hair. I could figure ways to glide my nails delicately along every steel surface I see, pick up parts with the tippy tip tip of my fingers. I could put the bolts in the overhead drop multiple as if they were rosebuds. I could pose like the Queen of Sheba every time I brought the multiple down on the oil pans, give it a few extra torques. Let them know I'm there.

Yes, I could figure out sizzling responses right then to all of their catcalls and jibes. But what's the use? There I was staring at myself in the dressing room mirror of Kara's Esquisite House of Beauté, and I feel their eyeballs rolling around on my skin like scoops of cold cantaloupe. I feel that bare. That stripped. Even that old dumpy wheezing committeeman couldn't feel worse than me right now. Even if he were stuck between the block washer and a crate of parts.

Death in the Sidesaddle

Henry Bivens shoved his Tigers cap on his head and left for work that morning feeling as fit as ever in his twenty-nine years at Cadillac, with one cup of coffee and a bowl of his wife's oatmeal under his belt to shore him up for his task of relieving eight jobs on the sidesaddle portion of the chassis line. He arrived early as usual to get eight pairs of clean gloves from his locked cabinet by the line and put them at the stations where he would begin relieving for morning break an hour after start of shift. A pair for Cooney, the one who loaded the frames at the beginning of the line, the first one he relieved before and after lunch. A pair for Georgette, the engine-mount-bracket lady. One for Frank on the upper control arms and a pair for the new kid on the shims job. Then Graciela, who tightened the control arm bolts. Roger on the frame brace job and Rufus who installed the lower control arm just before that crazy guy who ate garlic baloney sandwiches.

Garlic Baloney Joe always stuck his new, clean gloves in his back pocket and used the previous afternoon's gloves until lunchtime. That's when he turned the old pair in to Henry and whisked out the gloves he had received in the morning. His day didn't officially start until lunch, he told Henry, no matter what time General Motors tried to start him. Henry gave Joe a new pair of gloves every morning just the same, because in his opinion there was nothing in the morning like a fresh pair of gloves even though Georgette and Graciela complained religiously that clean, unbleached cotton gloves were too stiff for their fingers to grab bolts and parts. Whether they wanted them or not, no one in Henry's area, the first eight jobs on the front of the frame, ever had to scramble for a pair of gloves at 6:00 a.m. when the line jerked forward.

Henry waited for start of shift on top of the pallets that were an informal break area for almost everyone. The pallets had a sheet of cardboard over the top to protect against splinters. They butted up against a wall near the head of the line just around the corner from where the fully dressed engines from across the street dipped from the second floor to curve around and meet the frame at the top of the main chassis line. The air was thick with production noises trapped inside aluminum and steel machinery. The squeaks and moans and brrrrraps and taptaptaptaps and clinks and rrrrrrrrrs of final assembly waited inside still, absolutely still air guns, spring compressors, and hoists, straining to escape the aluminum or steel skins, the links of the line chains.

Big Fella, the three-legged rat, snuggled in his usual spot under the same set of pallets Henry sat atop. Big Fella's condition, caused by a careless forklift driver, had forced him to approach life more creatively; if he were to maintain his belly, he had to appeal to the benevolent side of his coworkers. Few would have claimed Big Fella as a coworker but, in truth, the four-legged, two-legged, and three-legged beings in that factory were all dependent on one master for survival. For a rat, factory living beat foraging in outdoor trash bins or suffering the traps of irate and stingy homeowners in the barrio around the plant. The alley rats that occasionally strayed into the plant were puny compared to Big Fella's magnificent brownish gray, foot-long body. From his hiding spot, he waited for a few crumbs from the peanut butter toast Henry nibbled.

Henry read in the morning paper about a little girl forced by her mother's boyfriend to march until she dropped dead while the mother looked on. Everyone would talk about that, thought Henry, asking each other again and again why women like that bear children. They would agree among themselves that a man like that should have his balls cut off. What is happening to this world that a human life means nothing, not even a child's? Henry shook his head because he had long suspected that human life means little. There have always been outright killings and slow murders. There will always be deaths that go against the grain of nature.

He learned this lesson from his father as he watched him die of black lung from the Harlan County coal mines. The smell of coal dust and rotting lungs wheezed out through his father's mouth and then the phlegm as he coughed, coughed, coughed. The stench of bile pooling at the top of his father's stomach permeated the house. They watched him stoop lower and lower until he couldn't get up from the bed by the kitchen woodstove. He needed warmth even though it was May and the dogwoods were in bloom. Then and there Henry made up his mind to head north away from the mines. At age twenty-five he hired in at Cadillac Motor Car Company on Clark Street.

One after the other they filed into the final assembly department. The rougher ones, the slouched ones, the determined ones kept walking until they reached the sidesaddle. When Garlic Baloney Joe bop/shuffled to his job, the air in the sidesaddle, already thick and funky, mixed unbearably with his baloney halitosis and the ooze of garlic and weed from his skin. Joe usually had his first hit of weed before he even dressed to come to work. And as soon as he flopped down at his job to wait for line start-up, he satisfied the weed hunger with a garlic baloney sandwich on a submarine bun, which he fixed from supplies he kept in his otherwise bare refrigerator at home. Joe was twenty-six and looked like an escapee from the Woodstock sixties with his long, straggly blond hair tied back with a rubber band, his scruffy beard, and his thin drug-infested body always in a slump. Half a second before the line started, Joe would mockingly survey the area through weed-laced eyes and bellow—Hey dudes, dudettes, are we ready? No one would respond. No one would talk to him for the rest of the day. The garlic kept his coworkers away from him and he seemed to like things that way. Joe's smell hung in the air worse after the curtains were installed.

Climate control in the sidesaddle was strictly in the hands of the weatherman in the years before Georgette and Graciela circulated a petition asking management to install heavy-duty plastic curtains. The sidesaddle, located by the railroad dock, had no doors at either end in order to facilitate unloading frames and other stock from the rail cars. The area was hot like every other spot in the plant during the summer but meat-freezer cold in the winter. Almost everyone on the line signed the petition except Joe, who rebuffed Georgette when she approached him. People on the line were angry at Joe for not signing and accused him of being so high all the time that he couldn't tell hot from cold.

The sidesaddle was the first line of the final assembly operation, officially part of the chassis line. The frame rode down the sidesaddle line differently than engines went down their lines or than the instrument panels went down their line. In all other areas, a unit went down the line front forward. In the sidesaddle the frames, black and coated with a protective tarry substance commonly called gook, went down the line sideways like railroad ties. People worked on the back and front of the frame at the same time instead of on the right and left sides as the rest of the plant did. People in that area claimed they rode the workhorse sidesaddle. They were a unique group because of working front and back simultaneously. That put a different kind of distance between them, a whole frame length instead of a frame width. A curious brand of individualism developed in the assemblers there. They seemed suspended in time, in the darkness of the area, around the corner from the rest of the department, away from each other but tied by the frames. It was difficult for even the most mature workers to feel stable in the area; the younger elements were total wild cards. All of these factors earned the area a reputation for being dirty because of the frame tar, heavy because of weighty suspension parts, and unpredictable because of its crew.

I ain't signing shit was what Joe said to Georgette. She ran back to Henry, who had given her an extra relief while she collected signatures, threw her hands on her plentiful Alabama hips, and cried that she was always sick because of this cold-assed area and the fool won't sign and I'm trying to do something to make it better for everyone. What's wrong with him?

Henry told Georgette to catch her job. He calmly went to Joe. One of the lessons Henry remembered from all the organizing drives he participated in as a coal miner's son was that there was something everyone would do to help the cause if approached properly. He also realized that signing a petition, making that black on white commitment, was too strong a move for some people. He said to Joe—it would help us a lot if you could just wear your coat and shiver a lot when the foreman walks by. Joe didn't say anything but he put his coat on about five minutes after Henry left him and shivered every time the foreman walked by. Later in the day, Joe slinked up to Georgette's station and scribbled his name on the petition.

The first day the climate control curtains hung, their plastic flaps dazzlingly clear and clean in contrast to the rest of the area, the left spring compressor broke loose. Jobs in the sidesaddle could be dangerous because there was always the possibility of dropping a control arm on a foot or cutting a limb on the frame, but no one expected the compressor to break loose and nearly kill Joe.

The compressor consisted of a three-and-a-half-foot-long piston suspended from an electric hoist with two large horseshoes on either end of it. The suspension spring, a black coil about eighteen inches high and nine inches in diameter at its widest, fit between the two horseshoes. When Joe pressed the button, the piston pulled the horseshoes together, causing them to squeeze the spring, which Joe could then slip between the upper and lower control arms. There were compression outfits for the right and left side of the front frame. Joe operated the left compressor.

The noise of the upper horseshoe breaking wasn't like two fingers snapping or bubble gum cracking or a balloon popping. It sounded like a circus cannon because the spring was under great compression. The noise startled everyone on the line from the frame loader at one end to the frame unloader at the other end. The horseshoe flew into the air across the railroad tracks and embedded itself into the concrete ceiling where it remains to this day. The spring released toward Joe, who barely got out of its way, bounced on a frame, and landed further down the line.

The spring job was the only one Joe had worked for the year he had been at Cadillac and he had done it without incident. But because they thought he was high all the time, those who worked around Joe blamed him for the accident. It wasn't until the union safety man investigated that everyone learned the compressor hadn't been checked in years for signs of wear and tear. A stress crack had developed where the horseshoe joined the piston, and it yielded moments before Henry was to relieve Joe for morning break.

The accident shocked Joe into sobriety. He repeated—I could've been killed. I could've been killed. Not only did he realize he could have lost his life through no fault of his own, it occurred to him that no one seemed to care. He felt the most alone he had ever felt in his life that day. Nearly killed and no one cared. Except Henry who patted Joe on the back and asked, hahya feeeeling? Henry had a way of talking slowly

and deliberately as if he were afraid people wouldn't understand his heavy Kentucky drawl. Hahya feeeeling, boy?

Only five minutes left until start of shift. First one and then
another straggler flew down the main aisle or ran in from the
Clark Street entrance across the railroad tracks, through the
entrance at the top of the line. The climate control curtains
were pulled back to allow in the early May air with its smell
of warm factory emissions. Garlic Baloney Joe examined his
spring compressor, tugged at both horseshoes, operated the
compressor button a couple of times. A careful equipment
inspection had become part of Joe's daily, sober routine since
the accident. Graciela and Georgette marched in together
down the main aisle giggling at an early morning compliment
from a hi-lo driver.

No one paid much attention to Henry, who still sat on the
pallet with the newspaper on his lap turned to part two of the
story about the little girl. Instead of newsprint, however, Henry
was seeing dogwood blooms just as if he were in Evart,
Kentucky, where just down the road from his boyhood home a
profusion of trees waved to the sky with their pale blossoms
tipped in the blood of Jesus. It was the dogwood crucified him,
his mother used to say. They made the sign of the cross when
his father died in his bed in the kitchen by the woodstove. His
mother, three brothers, four sisters, and him. They all heard the
low, pitiful intestinal growl from his father's spirit wanting to

be free. Henry heard that sound again that morning while he waited for the sidesaddle line to start. It was so loud and intimate that Henry doubted the sound could be coming from his recurring dream of his father's death. Was he dreaming? He was in the middle of a clump of dogwoods again. He couldn't figure out how or why but one tree jutted out of a box of upper control arm bolts. There was a tree by the frame loading hoist. He felt petals brush against his face from the tree by the engine overhead line. Henry wanted to smell the dogwood flowers. He had always wanted to smell them. He could never understand why such beautiful cream and red blossoms could be odorless.

Arrrrgh arrrrgh. Is he dead? Henry asked his mama that morning, is he dead? Aaaaaargh aaaargh aaaaargh and then nothing.

There is no breath, child, he's dead.

The line jumped forward at six sharp with an abnormal metallic clang, as if it had run into itself. Joe looked up, startled by the noise. What happened? Then he realized there had been no hahya feeeeling, boy? Joe looked at Henry who usually puttered about as the line started. Henry, Henry he called out. There was no movement.

Hey dudes, dudettes. Hey dudes, dudettes. Hey dudes, dudettes. As loud as he could yell, his head thrown back. Dudes, dudettes.

What the fuck you want, Baloney? Rufus responded after realizing that Joe had extended his usual morning outcry.

Henry, Henry . . . he ain't moving. It took a long time for Joe to speak because he wasn't used to saying anything to anyone except Henry, and Henry wasn't moving. There was no hahya feeeeling, boy? No one else ever asked Joe how he was feeling. In his whole life no one asked Joe how he felt about anything, not his mother who drowned herself in the bottle, not his father who he never saw, not his older brother who was busy becoming a success in order to escape their upbringing.

Henry? Joe yelled.

Everyone within reach of Joe's voice stopped what they were doing and stared at Henry sitting on the stack of wooden pallets, leaned up against the wall with his eyes wide open and a big smile under his deep black bushy mustache.

Maybe he's resting, said Georgette.

Maybe he had a hard night, snickered Frank.

Henry Henry, yelled Rufus. My God, he's not moving.

Joe left his job and double-stepped over to Henry and saw the wetness between his legs and the puddle trickling from under the pallet; it came to meet the toe of Joe's right cowboy boot. Joe just stood there not moving one muscle, hardly breathing and not because of the smell that began emanating from Henry but because he saw a blankness on Henry's face he had never seen before, a stillness in his normally lively, small frame. Joe recognized death even though he had never seen it before. He had never had a friend die. He had never had a friend. A long tear streamed from his left eye.

Someone went for the line foreman, who took one look at Henry and said—Oh my God—and ran to the office to phone for the general foreman, Ripowski, known as Ripoff behind his back. It had never occurred to the line foreman to call the medical department because he instinctively knew Henry was dead. He could see the looseness of the body, hands flopped to the side, palm up, and the frozen smile. He could see that Henry's chest was not moving. He saw the stream of water escaping from the pallet and concluded that it was the last urine. The foreman was new and automatically assumed that his boss should be the first notified if an employee died on site.

Ripowski, a big man, pushed his way through the group gathered around Henry's peaceful body. What's going on here? Call medical. Tell them to bring a stretcher. I can see his chest rising. Look. He placed a mirror he had brought under Henry's nose. There's breath, he bellowed. There's breath. There's breath they whispered in the group until the message reached Cooney who had stopped the line when Rufus yelled, my God, he's not moving. Ripowski yelled, start up that goddam line. There's breath.

Down the line it echoed. There's breath brrrrap brrrrrrap, taptaptaptap, rrrrrrrrr. There's breath, meeeearp meeeeearp. There's breath; grab that brake line.

After medical retrieved the body, the foreman ushered the hi-lo drivers and cleaners back to work. o.k. folks that's all for today. Let's get back to work, he said, his voice stiff.

AUTOPSY OF AN ENGINE

The foreman was still trying to reconcile what he really saw with Ripowski's instructions. Get him out of here. Let them declare him dead at the hospital. Why the hell do these people have to die here? Makes the company look bad; it's bad for insurance liability. I'll explain later. Ripowski whispered this while placing his hand on the foreman's shoulder as if welcoming him to the supervisory brotherhood. Get someone to clean up the mess and get yourself a cup of coffee.

The foreman barked out instructions in a tone everyone recognized as different from his usual benign approach. But he needed his job just like they needed theirs. The shock of Henry's death pushed him over into hard-line supervision at least for that moment. Clean up this mess. Move these pallets. Hey Joe, get your ass back on the job.

Joe shuffled back to his station and watched as a crew of cleaners spread speedy-dry on the pool of urine to soak it up. One of them, a friend of Henry's, grabbed Henry's lunch pail, newspaper, and Tigers baseball cap and placed it on his cleaning truck. Then a hi-lo driver came along to move the pallets. Joe saw the large wet spot on the cardboard that covered the top pallet. As the pallets were lifted by the two forks of the hi-lo, a cleaner stood by ready to apply more speedy-dry to the last bit of Henry that would ever be inside the Cadillac plant.

With the pallets removed, those closest saw Big Fella lying there just as peaceful as Henry had, his body parallel to the flow of urine. Big Fella's body attracted as much attention as

Henry's, if not more because everyone was able to get a good, leisurely look at him. Dead, Big Fella looked like any other factory rat. With his three legs tucked up under his body, no one could tell he was an amputee until the cleaner poked him with his broom and Big Fella flopped over.

I'll be goddam, said Cooney. You s'pose that rat checked out when Henry did?

That question teased a nervous twitter from almost everyone. Poor Henry. They all shook their heads one by one in a ripple of sympathy down the line. Poor Henry. Everyone knew Henry died right in that plant with the newspaper in his lap and his face smiling at all the people he had relieved for sixteen years.

The folks around Joe felt sorry for him because they could see he was hurt. They began to catch his job for him. In times of tragedy like that, factory people had a way of closing around each other, picking up the pieces, forgetting how they might argue during normal times. That was the case then. Everyone around Joe picked up bits and pieces of his job because they realized Henry's death had affected him in ways that didn't need probing right then and there.

Joe was in a fog wondering if some of Henry had soaked through the oil-coated floors and was trapped in the factory forever. Would Henry's spirit ever be free of the plant because the general foreman wouldn't declare him dead? No matter what was going on in Joe's head, the folks who worked around him were willing to welcome Joe from that day forward into the sidesaddle as truly one of them, garlic baloney and all.

Cooney placed his hand on Joe's shoulder. It's all right man; it's all right.

Just then Joe saw the dead rat and something in him snapped. He tore away from Cooney's touch and ran down the aisle gesticulating like a madman, his ponytail flying, crying out—the rat's dead. The rat's dead. He ran past the chassis line where the frame hung front to rear until he reached the hub of final assembly where there were the most lights in the whole department, where the body drop operation, the final repair, and the drive-away areas intersected. He rotated in the hub as if riding a twirl-a-loop and yelled again. Then he ran back up the aisle toward the sidesaddle which formed the top of a T in relation to the rest of the chassis line. Cooney met him at the beginning of the main chassis line and tried to stop Joe from hooking a left toward the lower Scotten Avenue exit door. Cooney didn't want Joe to get fired. Joe stopped a minute, breathless, pulled his gloves out of his back pocket and slammed them to the ground. Fuck this shit. Fuck all of you. I ain't dying in this place. I ain't dying in here. I ain't.

And Joe ran past the Scotten guard shack, down the road, past the parking lot, leaving everyone in his area wondering who would give them a break since the only spare man who could have replaced Henry that morning would have to cover Joe's job.

Thanks to Abbie Wilson

Everyone had their way of saying good-bye to the motor line. With Abbie it was pound cakes. She baked twenty-five of them for the final day. Almost everyone followed the job to Livonia, a Detroit suburb, except those close to retirement, those with medical restrictions, and Abbie Wilson, who didn't take to change easily. But she brought pound cakes for everyone to eat. Take them home, she said. Take them to the new job in the suburbs. It was what she knew how to do. Bake pound cakes. That's what she took out of Hernando, Mississippi. It was what kept her a husband until he died.

In those weeks after the motor line moved, Abbie wandered every day up and down the aisles at break through the block-test area. The lights were bright. Things were still set up as if people were about to enter each job space, grab a gun, some bolts, and make an engine. But only tradesmen arrived little by little to remove overhead lines, take up the floorboards, and rip out the engine turnover. Soon the front-and-oil-pan multiple air guns and the spark-plug guns were gone. The block washer at the top of line one, gone. The engine cold-start fuel and exhaust lines, gone. The coffee machine, gone. Then all the shipping dock men disappeared. One day Abbie wandered through on break from her new job cleaning third-floor manufacturing offices and there were no lights. She walked until she didn't know where she was walking anymore. Everything was gone, dark, no reference points.

It wasn't easy for a fortyish Abbie to begin working anywhere after her husband's death, especially in a big-time automobile plant, but the motor line was something else when Abbie entered its world in 1967. She spent her first few weeks on afternoons bolting down the engine front plate with a big, black boxy air gun with eight sockets called the multiple. During breaks she wandered to other parts of the plant and discovered that there was no other area like lines one, two, and three. Together they were the motor line, the main component of the engine build process. People were jam-packed, sweaty, oozing juicy energy and funk assembling those big cast-iron 472 engines. Something about building 472s. Everyone revved up. Not like trying to build a lightweight aluminum engine in the suburb. People might have hired in gentle or scared, or with ideas about how life should be, or might not have any spirit, didn't want to look anything in the face and dare it, but in department 1308, the motor line, folks acquired a whole lot of soul when those 472s were through with them.

All that shifting of products and processes from one space to another, that was progress. That was magic. From parts storage and shipping came the presses to create parts. After the black belch of the foundry ovens, sleek new Eldorados hummed off the line. Brand new configurations, engineering dreams, manufacturing miracles.

Abbie wasn't anyone's mother or daughter or sibling or niece outside the plant. Inside she was known as the quiet lady with the pound cakes. Curry was the one who understood Abbie and told everyone to be patient with her; she was trying to figure things out. That's how country girls are. Slow at first. It takes them a while; so they just go with the flow.

That was it. Abbie went with the flow. When the line started she started. When it stopped she stopped. When Gary put in the front-plate bolts, she tightened them. If the afternoon person on Abbie's job left her fifteen pieces of stock, she left fifteen. If everyone worked she worked. If everyone stopped she sat down, too. Because of stopping and starting and sitting and standing when everyone else did, there were times she didn't feel like she was just Abbie. There were times she felt like she was a bunch of folks all at once. It was when she was a bunch of folks all at once that Abbie was able to lose her loneliness, blend in better, smile like the rest, contribute pound cakes to line or department parties. That's how Abbie got to be called Cousin Cake from 1308.

On the first Monday the department was completely stripped, she stood in the aisle between lines one and two and stared for fifteen minutes at a time in each direction to see if one of the multiples had left its outline. She stepped twenty of her feet from Curry's old elevator door, casually as if she had one or two minutes left on break, before Abbie realized her body was turned wrong. She should have seen the edge of the freestanding elevator from the corner of her right eye at seven paces. Instead, she felt the elevator's squareness absolutely to the right of her. She was functioning on blind powers. The bastards didn't leave one stinking light.

Fifty paces away from the back elevator, Curry's route every morning with the latest jokes and rumors. Friday morning was cake day. A fresh one for him. What did his wife think? Fifty paces and Abbie was at the oil gasket installation fixture on line number one, only five steps from where she actually flipped the pans onto the upside down engine.

Five steps to the right and she was at Gertha's job. Four to the left was Vernell's. That was when Abbie moved slowly. When she sped up to cover Gertha's job or Vernell's or Mattie's while one of them went to the ladies' room, Abbie found herself almost a job and a half toward the head of the line if she installed Gertha's oil pump or clear down to the end of the line almost in Bill-the-engine-turnover-man's lap if she was loading Vernell's oil-pan-drop multiple gun. Also from the multiple she could gaze across the aisle to line number two and see Mario, the hi-lo driver who delivered her stock, darting from one job to another whispering in women's ears, especially Rosa's.

She squinted her eyes hoping to spot a figure dance up to a line, back away a few paces, wait a minute, move up to the line again, back a few paces, and so on as if installing a part. Then Abbie closed her eyes completely and listened for the sound of a hi-lo crashing a parts rack to the floor. She sniffed the air for the choking, nauseating smoke from a gasoline hi-lo. That was how Abbie tried to define the big empty space that was once the motor line. Finally, she noticed something that she had never paid attention to in all her years at Cadillac. The support posts in the plant had numbers and letters on them corresponding to each department. Motor line letters were in the latter part of the alphabet. A motor line series might be: U1, U2, V8, V9. There were two sets facing each other: U1 on one post. A space in between. U1 on another post. Then on the other side of the post, U2. A space in between. Another U2. U3 on the other side of that U2 and so on. Abbie asked her new boss in the cleaning department what the letters and numbers meant. Bays, he said. Those are bay numbers. A hi-lo driver might deliver parts to bay U1. Then the foreman might tell him to check the parts supply in bay U7. Got that, Abbie?

Yeah, got it. She had worked in bay v8. She stared at that empty space as if she were in a trance. Then she nodded her head slowly and smiled broadly. Oil pan bay, she said. I worked in oil pan bay. She threw her hands on her hips defiantly as if she, Abbie Wilson, were now in control of the motor line, as if that motor line were her kitchen and she was about to get things cooking.

Abbie walked up and down line number one, now with one hand on her hips while she pointed to the old work stations. This is crank bay, she said. And this is Fabulous Freddie's bay. Abbie continued to walk, punctuating each renaming with a bob of her head. This is Gertha Bay. Turnover Bay. Abbie liked the sound of the bay names so she renamed her job Pound Cake Bay. Everyone would know there was more than just oil pans going on in Pound Cake Bay.

Having renamed the bays on line one, Abbie stood near the old multiple area. From that position she could peep around the coffee machines and the head of whomever was sitting at the snack table and see the men on the shipping and receiving dock. Sometimes they were all standing in the entrance between the dock and 1308. At other times, the dock men fanned out to various social spots on the motor line like the beginning of the bend in line two where Alberta used to install the carburetor, and all the men buzzed like flies trying to get a date with her. Abbie named that spot Moonlight Bay.

Times when Abbie wasn't moving up and down the line, she settled in the middle of her job area and between installing oil pans, stared into space. Those were the times when Abbie felt like she was standing in a perfectly dry bubble in the middle of the noise and sweat but she was calm, cool, and breathing spring air. She could hear it then. Another kind of noise, other conversations from another time, and she felt as if she were in another place.

She used to feel that way when she was a little girl, ten or so, going to daylong Sunday services in Hernando. Everyone she knew was in that church on Sunday except the white store owners. The congregation sang and clapped and prayed and testified even on hot days when the church was a sweaty mist. But Abbie always cleared a space for herself to breathe. Something would seep into her that she couldn't define. She felt possessed by cucumber coolness while waiting for fellowship after the services and a piece of her mother's pound cake.

That same kind of coolness possessed Abbie on Tuesday, the day after she reestablished her old work station and renamed the bays. At lunchtime she carefully rolled the hand truck carrying her trash drum and other janitorial supplies out of the office area into the hallway by the women's locker room and left it there. She descended two flights of stairs to the motor line with her lunch box and an old stool, shuffled over fifty years of oil-caked floor and headed for Pound Cake Bay where she had eaten lunch her first twelve years at Cadillac.

Just like the old days. Half an hour to the second after beginning lunch Abbie stood, brushed off some crumbs from her sandwich, looked up and down the area, and waited as if the line would start rolling at any moment. It began as a simple recall exercise for Abbie. How did I used to do that job? She went through the motions, slowly at first, pretending to lift an oil pan from a pretend rack. She installed pretend rubber gaskets on each end of the pretend pan and swung the pan onto a pretend engine. Then she reached for another pan, another set of rubber gaskets. She flipped the pan on another engine. Some things never leave you, she said out loud. It's like riding a bike.

Abbie lifted pans, installed gaskets, and threw the pans on the engines until she wasn't pretending anymore. Her muscles began to ache around the shoulders and forearms. She could hear the thud of the oil pan as it met with the engine. She could hear the whiz of the drop multiple as the oil pan was tightened. She could hear the whoosh thump of the engine as it flipped in the turnover and left the line. You are one bad sister, she said, working until she was dog tired. But it felt good to be useful again.

From then on she headed for the oil pan job every lunch break to work until she made the engines come down the line and the oil pans flop on the upside-down blocks. She didn't have to reorient herself from Curry's elevator anymore. She knew where to install pan gaskets and where to put the pans on the engine. Each day she added a new bay according to which areas her eyes spotted during the normal course of doing her job. In this way she added Cam Bay, Pretty Man's Bay, Easy Money Bay. She created the whole block area behind her because all she had to do was turn her head over her left shoulder when she was at the oil pan gasket fixture. Then she could see the maze of table-level lines with blocks rolling on them, heading for the top of her line for crank and piston installation.

On Wednesday her eyes fell to the right of her, northeast of her job. She saw Fabulous Freddy on number four piston, not shooting it hard the way the others shot theirs, but easing it in gently, gracefully like a ballet dancer. First he took number four from the tray by the block, stepped back from the line, and bent his body slightly while coaxing the piston into the ring-compressing sleeve. His shoulders hunched while he slipped piston and sleeve into the cylinder. He positioned the installer at the cylinder, took a step back, brought himself to his full six feet, swiveled his hips, pulled the installer handle down, and schoop the piston sailed into the chamber while Freddy pivoted and landed with rod cap and nuts in hand to complete the job. Then on to the next engine and the next number four. She hardly ever spoke to Freddy in the old days. She was shy and he was so much younger than her. But on the day she rediscovered him on piston number four, Abbie couldn't help herself. She waved.

Hey Freddy, I got some pound cake for you.

The next day Abbie brought in a pound cake and left it for Freddy on a railing close to the piston section. That day she also found words to talk to Vernell like she never could before. In the past, Abbie knew Vernell had eyes for Curry and would get upset when Curry spent more time talking to Abbie than her. Abbie wondered herself why Curry spent so much time with her because in her eyes Vernell was a beauty: copper skin, brick-house figure, bright-colored blouses over her jeans with makeup to match. Vernell smelled like a perfume counter even at end of shift when Abbie reeked like used socks. In Vernell's eyes Abbie was one of those backward, no-shaped women who spent Sundays in church and fried chicken for wakes. Neither one of them understood that Curry simply liked to joke and talk. Nothing else. Neither one of them ever realized that Curry was the quiet center of his section of the plant, the one who welcomed and unofficially oriented all the newcomers as he had Abbie. He was the one the old-timers went to for memories, the one the foremen sought for advice.

Abbie decided that day to overcome old tensions and tell Vernell how much she has missed Curry since his death a year before the motor line moved. While Abbie was explaining her feelings to Vernell, an over-the-road driver who traveled between the downtown Detroit plant and its suburban extension wandered into Abbie's department and couldn't believe his eyes. It was the first time he had been in the area since the motor line moved. He was shocked in the same way that Abbie was. He walked up and down the aisles. The multiple air guns and spark plug guns were gone. The block washer at the top of line one, gone. The engine cold-start fuel and exhaust lines, gone. The coffee machines, gone. All of the people he once visited in the department were gone. There were no lights. Everything was gone, dark, no reference points.

Then he saw Abbie. From where he stood she looked as if she was performing a ritual or a dance. She swiveled, bent, raised her hands, turned again, raised her hands again, moved forward, moved back. He watched in fascination for almost fifteen minutes. He watched and watched, as you would in a movie, until he felt as if he were a part of whatever she was doing. Soon he began hearing a noise, a buzzing. Then a whirring. Then braap braap. Then he heard the buzzing, the whirring, the braaping all at once as if in concert. Soon the whole department seemed to be hopping. For a half an hour a workforce buzzed and machinery hummed.

He left and returned a few minutes later with a buddy who used to work in department 1308 driving hi-los. Just watch that lady over there, he said to his friend. And it happened for his friend the way it happened for him. The two walked up and down the main aisle wordless. What could they say? Abbie saw them and waved. Of course, they saw Abbie, too, but didn't realize she was waving at them because by this time they thought Abbie was part of the scene, the reenactment, the film. They didn't know what it was.

After that day, others began to trickle into 1308 to see again what they had experienced before. They came after their day shift was over in Livonia or before they reported for work in the afternoon. They stopped in after conducting business at the Cadillac Credit Union up the street. They tiptoed in one by one or a few at a time, afraid others would think they were crazy, but they came. And those who observed Abbie long enough were able to see themselves. They were amazed and happy because they all looked so young, energetic, and hopping in a way they hadn't for years. Abbie waved at them because she knew they were happy to see themselves at their best when struggles with the bosses and each other were at their hottest, when Peanut Man hawked hot roasteds all through the shift, when Sweet Sadie sold her blouses and jewelry, when Red took liquor orders for lunch, when Thanksgiving was one long banquet of tamales and greens, and Dancing John, dressed up as Santa Claus, drove his jitney on the last day of work before Christmas break singing ho, ho, ho we'll soon be out the doh.

Even Foreman Smith, nicknamed Pillsbury because he was pasty white, squat, and round, snuck in to see if what he had heard was true. He caught Crazy Marge cussing him out like she always did. You Pillsbury Doughboy muthafucka you. Foreman Smith, the Pillsbury Doughboy, reached in his pocket, pulled out a handkerchief and cried and cried and cried, not because it was cathartic facing his past, but because he saw Abbie's pound cake. It reminded him that no matter how many muthafuckas Crazy Marge called him, there was a strong family in 1308, and he was part of it.

For another week members of the family came to see the old motor line and took a piece of cake. Abbie had stopped leaving cake on railings. She had found a box and dragged it to the main aisle, put a small tablecloth over it, a vase with an orange silk flower and began leaving the cake there in a Tupperware container. Pretty soon people left notes. Thank you, thank you for everything. Thanx for the cake. Are you that cake lady? GM sure is great to do this for us, said one. There were always those who didn't understand, but Abbie collected each note for her scrapbook.

Abbie took immense pleasure in seeing the old faces even though they didn't realize she was really alive in the scene. They ate her cakes and communicated through the thank-you notes. Abbie had become so absorbed with her accomplishment she completely forgot that Curry hadn't visited. Maybe the time schedule was wrong. He was, after all, on midnights and gone by eight or 8:30 a.m. Abbie could only work the line in the afternoons between 11:00 a.m. and 3:30 p.m. when her own shift ended. In the morning she had to clean offices. Abbie decided to leave a cake for Curry. She had done that the first few weeks after the line left but that was out of desperation. She had no plan, no power. No reason really to leave cakes. The rats ate them. Abbie believed that things were different now, that Curry could eat the cake like all the other visitors. It never occurred to her that Curry was dead and beyond all magic she could weave with her mind, her body, her pound cakes.

Abbie stayed up all night baking a slightly larger than normal cake. She covered it with butter frosting and carefully wrote in red and blue decorating glaze, TO MY BEST FRIEND CURRY. She reported to the plant the next day earlier than her 7:00 a.m. start time and left the cake on a box by the elevator. At lunchtime, she checked. There was no note, only chunks missing from the edge. She removed the cake, wrapped it, and threw it away. The next morning, she presented another cake to the elevator, larger with red and yellow flowers and the same message, TO MY BEST FRIEND CURRY. At lunchtime, there were nibbles on the edge and a rat path through the middle.

Abbie completed the rest of the shift in her motor line department in the middle of Pound Cake Bay while Fabulous Freddy danced, Mario flirted, and Vernell switched her brick-house body from one end of the multiple to the other. But Abbie didn't say a word. At three-thirty she collected the box by the elevator, the box in the middle of the aisle, the Tupperware container, the vase and orange flower, and a few notes left that day by people she didn't notice because she had been so preoccupied.

At home that evening she soaked her aching muscles in a tub of Epsom salts for three hours after which she showered away any remaining oily sweat and grimy memories. Then she went to church that Sunday to beg forgiveness for playing God, for hoping to defy the laws of nature. She never returned to the motor line area on Clark Street. She avoided first-floor manufacturing when arriving or leaving her job on the third floor even when the company renovated the area to accommodate a shrunken hi-lo repair department and a storage area for unsold Cadillac Allantes.

Several years after Abbie's recreation of the motor line, car production ceased at the plant. Five years after that, the company announced the closing of plating, the last operation at the Clark Street Plant. All production would cease there. No machines would ever groan at Clark Street again. Only a token crew of tradesmen and cleaners would remain. Abbie didn't know if she would survive the final closing and keep a job. She returned from church the Sunday after the announcement and immediately reported to the kitchen. She began baking cakes. One, two, three, four—pound cake after pound cake after pound cake. She stacked them on her kitchen table. They spilled over to the dining and living rooms. There were pound cakes on the stairs leading to the second floor of her colonial. There were cakes in her spare bedroom, pound cakes in the linen closet, and pound cakes in the hallway outside her bedroom. When she had baked until she could bake no longer, Abbie cleared a spot on her couch, grabbed the scrapbook from under the coffee table, and found the thank-you notes she had never read. One was from Vernell. Abbie, are you still around? Your cakes are as good as ever.

Another note said, *mil gracias*. She knew that was from Mario even though she didn't know what *mil* meant. She knew *gracias* when she saw it. That was Mario. Too bad she missed him, she thought. When he delivered oil pans to her, he used to help her pull them down if they were stacked too high. He was the only driver who did that. In return she listened to his romance problems. He asked her advice as if she knew something about romance. He equated age with wisdom and knowledge even about things never experienced. *Mil gracias,* he wrote, you are still my favorite *mujer*. *Gracias a Dios* for people like you.

There was another note. It said, thanks to Abbie Wilson. Just like that, thanks to Abbie Wilson. Abbie took a deep breath while her face filled with hot moisture that at first boiled in her abdomen, traveled through her shoulders and fingertips, swirled in her chest, then gushed from her eyes, nose, and mouth. Abbie's head weaved nearly out of control. How could it be? She asked over and over. She lifted her head to the ceiling and stretched up her hand with the note in it as if the answer to her question could trickle down her arm into her heart. She knew the handwriting. There was no mistaking the scrawl. How could she have missed that one last visit? Thanks to Abbie Wilson, the note said. I had one more taste of life. Your best friend, Curry.

The Last Car

On any other day, the cobalt blue Fleetwood body would rest unattended on a trestle at the edge of the second floor, its sides smudged with assembly fingerprints, its windshield taped with assembly instructions called broadcast sheets. Already fitted with an instrument panel, seats, a headliner, internal lighting, and wiring harnesses, it would wait for descent to the final assembly line to unite with the engine and chassis, the hood and fenders, headlights. Then oo la la. It would become a Cadillac Fleetwood Brougham.

At any other time, the final transformation from assorted parts and systems to car would happen quickly. In an instant. A push of the body over the second-floor edge where, tucked in its special hoist, it would hover no longer than a few seconds. And WHOOUMP. The car would come together: a body from the Fleetwood plant with a Cadillac chassis and engine. A door painted at Fleetwood, Cadillac's sister plant, a mile down the Interstate 75 corridor, united with the bumper from the Cadillac plating department. Just like that. A flick of the operator's thumb and the hoist delivered. Whoooump. From second floor, smacko, right on the money to four young men in the pit, under the chassis, with guide drifts ready to ease the body on.

But on the morning of December 18, 1987, the time that it took for the cobalt blue Brougham to become a car was measured in seconds that became minutes and minutes that stretched as long as first-floor final assembly. Time bounced from the man who loaded the frame onto the sidesaddle. It passed through the woman who installed the shocks. It rolled over and under the men who loaded the gas tank. And stopped for who knows how long at the body drop area where the press of the crowd observing the final glorious moments of car assembly at Cadillac Motor Car Company, Clark Street, Detroit, delayed the body's drop.

Over a period of years, Cadillac models were nibbled away from Clark Street. First Eldorado and Seville relocated. Next the de Ville left town. Then the last Fleetwood, cobalt blue with diamond twinkles wherever the light hit, simulated convertible top, and light blue leather interior. In an eye blink it was there. In another eye blink the Cadillac assembly at its original home was history.

That morning, second-floor workers hustled around the body making unusual preparations for the drop. They patted its ample luxury car sides one last time with their gloved hands. They gently tugged at the electronically loaded instrument panel; punched the front seats top, middle, bottom until they achieved the right depression in the cushions; took their gloves off for a real feel of the velvety-soft leather interior; picked up scraps of paper, bits of thread from the carpeting. Someone buffed a fingerprint from the driver's door. Another retrieved a stray instrument panel screw from the door molding. Three or four coworkers helped the hoist operator pull the mammoth hoist over the body. This was normally a solo job, but everyone wanted a piece of the last action that day. A cluster of workers performed checks on the hoist itself to ensure that it wrapped around the body securely. They yanked at its heavy, steel bars, four on either side. They passed their hands over the carpeted arms that locked under the lip of the body. One last look up at the network of chains and pulleys controlling the hoist. One last long sniff inside and out of the car. Then the hoist operator grabbed the controls in his right hand. The second-floor crew helped him push the body off the trestle and into the dangling space a floor above its destination. Everyone crowded around the edge of the second floor. A few, those most intimately involved with the final second-floor preparations, held hands. Workers from all over the plant leaned over the railings, wondering what would become of their jobs in the plant-wide shakedown that would follow the closing of assembly. Salaried personnel already began to miss the lights and noise they would encounter in the assembly area en route from one set of offices to another. Poor assembly workers, they speculated, what will become of them? It hadn't occurred to them yet that there would be changes in their lives as well.

Then all waited as if the drop could proceed as usual, with the hoist operator visually aligning the body in the air and the frame on the conveyor. They stood there viewing the rear of the body and its sides through the orange bars of the hoist. Their grips on each other's hands tightened. Their eyes focused on the chassis below. It would happen at any moment. This is it. This is it. Hold it. Hold it. One, two. This is it, this is it, this is it. No, not yet. Take a deep breath. Hold it. Hold it. Hold it.

Everyone hadn't arrived yet at the first-floor body drop. Droves of onlookers were still converging on the area. Mechanics and salaried technicians came from the Engineering Building. Cleaners and sweepers from every corner of the plant, stock people from Merritt Warehouse, clerks and secretaries from the administration building, top-level Cadillac management, and all the union representatives, those who were not at a Las Vegas UAW conference. WKBX television station was there.

The second-to-the-last frame had already met its chassis but languished in the station after the body drop. It could not complete its transformation until the last body fell and the conveyor began moving again. The brown Brougham was designated for a Fleetwood worker. Free raffle tickets had been distributed to assemblers at both plants for a chance at the last two cars. A Cadillac worker, part of the workforce that married the body to the Cadillac frame, installed the Cadillac engine, Cadillac gas tank, brakes, exhaust system, suspension, electronic systems, would win the last car to roll off the line on Clark Street. Ever.

Were it a typical day, things would have been relatively quiet, almost lifeless. The work day in final assembly usually began as a slow dream. Sleepy figures donned aprons, wet their gloves with cold fountain water to ensure a good fit, and shuffled papers at inspection sites. Young men walked toward one of several trenches in the conveyor, slid down an edge, and disappeared. At fifty-four cars an hour, shiny Cadillacs rolled off the line with monotonous, relentless regularity. At any point after the chassis transferred from its assembly line and the body dropped onto it from the second floor, some tired soul would set a pair of gloves on fire and stuff them into the conveyor or chuck a broom handle in there, anything to stop the line, get a rest. Some days each car passed with a prayer for a few extra seconds break whispered behind it. That was the concept of factory time: seconds were minutes, minutes were hours, hours were forever.

Early in the shift on the last day, the strains of what became a processional chorus first arose spontaneously from the dock by the railroad tracks on lower Clark as the workers there observed the dwindling stack of frames. It moved as a feeble hum a few feet along to the sidesaddle area, the beginning phase of first-floor assembly. It shaped itself into vocal utterances as two men hooked the last frame and positioned it onto the sidesaddle conveyor. When the two frame loaders completed their job, they doffed their gloves and followed the frame. This routine was repeated by the other assemblers on the first half of the sidesaddle line. By the time they arrived at the control arms station, the song burst forth loud and strong from the lips of the fifteen or so people who were following the frame. Na na naa naaaa. Na na naa naaaa. Hey-hey-hey . . . goooood-bye. It was as if the line was folding up in the frame's wake. The pattern continued down the rest of the sidesaddle. As each person finished a job, the group grew larger and louder. Na na naa naaaa. Hey-hey-hey . . . goooood-bye. Install the brake lines, walk. Tighten the frame brace, walk. While the frame transferred from the sidesaddle to the chassis line, the chorus, which by then included nearly the entire sidesaddle line, dock workers, and strays from other areas on that end of the building, positioned themselves in the aisle at the head of the chassis line and began harmonizing as if they were Christmas carolers.

A woman in full Santa Claus regalia joined the group at that point. She worked on the sidesaddle conveyor installing fuel lines. After completing her job, she slipped on the Santa outfit she had rented for the day in an attempt to make the best of what everyone realized was a bad situation. Her Nestlé's chocolate face, framed by the white fuzz on her red hat, smiled bravely as she added her voice to the caroling. By virtue of her costume, she became the conductor. She faced the carolers confidently, waved her arms stiffly. And a one. And a two. And na na naa naaaa. Na na naa naaa. Hey-hey-hey . . . goooood-bye. Thus, she assumed leadership of the procession when it rejoined the frame at the head of the chassis line and led her coworkers throughout the first half of the line until the group arrived at the gas-tank station.

That was where the procession lost its composure. Whatever religious, incantatory, spiritual mood had developed from the increasingly loud and fervent repetition of the old rock and roll refrain, dissolved once someone yelled, Let's sign the tank. Everyone instantly produced magic markers and began affixing their names to the tank, which at that point, swung from four chains until it would be permanently fastened after the body drop. A group hunched over the tank, scribbled names, dates, a heart, a smile. Another group replaced the first, which shifted to the outer edge of the action. Then another would rotate inward while the other rotated out. Then another in. And another out.

In this way the chassis progressed toward the body drop, still at normal line speed but surrounded by a throbbing blob of people, all trying to sign the tank. At times, only an arm could pierce through a group around the chassis in order to scratch its mark on the tank. Foremen signed. General foremen signed. Secretaries from the administration building squeezed their way through and penned their names. The head of security, the head of medical, the head of personnel, the head of the whole Clark Street operation signed.

It was the act of signing the tank that pulled the emotional plug in the department, releasing a flow of tears, hugs, kisses, and fervent well-wishes such as had never been experienced on Clark Street, even when the motor line left for Livonia several years before. Some signed carefully, as if the curves of their n's or o's, the slant of their t's or l's on the cold gray tank, would mystically ensure that their past, as assemblers of America's foremost luxury cars, also would be their future. Others scrawled their names as if the gas tank would link them to each other forever.

—Hey, Niño, what are you going to do when this is over?

—I'm headed home to Tejas, baby. Me and my old man we're going to open up a *taquería* in San Antonio.

—Well come here, baby, and give Big Mama a hug and kiss. I don't know when I'll ever see you again.

At last, frame and followers converged on the body drop, joining the throng there. The press of people was so great that there was a danger someone would fall into the pit from where workers were trying valiantly to emerge in order to reach the top of the tank. The headlight checkers and final inspection people attempted to squeeze through for their signatures, as did the repairmen at the extreme end of the department. Last minute signers and onlookers pushed around the chassis to such a degree that plant security was unable to maneuver its way through to help control the crowd. In desperation several supervisors, already in the area, and a few line workers linked their outstretched hands on either side of the chassis in order to keep people away long enough for the body to drop.

The tension on the second floor mounted as the hoist operator held his thumb poised over the down button. He had been holding it in that position so long that he lost all sensation in his thumb. He wiggled it to ensure that it was still in working order. Day after day for five years he had dropped bodies at the correct moment without a hitch, almost by instinct. Now he must wait for a signal.

Those around him began to close ranks as others arrived to join in. The hand grips grew tighter, their knuckles grew paler. Whew, the broadcast lady said. This suspense is killing me, and she weaved her head a few times and gently wiggled her body as if casting off a spell. Whew, yeah. Ain't that the truth. Others echoed her sentiment. More heads rotated to loosen up the neck muscles. A few broke their hand grips long enough to flex their fingers, get the blood flowing again, and then they reconnected tighter than before. Their faces were blank, absolutely expressionless as the eyes of those on the second floor locked with those on the first, creating a time tunnel, a kind of spiritual corridor through which the last body would travel.

The signal for the drop would come at any moment as those on the first floor craned their necks upward at the body nestled so sweetly in its orange steel cradle while carpeted hooks caressed its underside. The onlookers began wrapping arms around each other's waists. They were already body to body, pressed so tightly that a sheet of onionskin paper couldn't slide between. You could hear a screw drop. You could hear paper fall. You could hear a rat breathe at that moment.

Then the members of the chain blockading the chassis looked at each other, sweat popping off their faces. The foreman of the body drop was transported by the intensity of the historical moment. He freed his hands from the chain and surveyed the area, fixing his eyes first on this one, then on another, as if he had been imbued by some special power. But the crowd was already frozen, waiting for the drop. He lifted his arms dramatically from his sides. It was, after all, one of the rare times he had to directly intervene in the timing of a body drop. The hoist operator and the pit crew were able to manage the drop themselves in the past. He began waving his arms in opposing circles, a movement vaguely reminiscent of his days in the navy, then flung his right arm magisterially and pointed to the body in midair. That was it. That was it. One, two. The hoist operator took one last long breath, wiggled his thumb one last time, and WHOOUP. Yes. Yes. That was it.

It all went by so fast, really, once the hoist operator received the signal to push the button. Eighteen days later, on the Feast of the Epiphany, there would be little left in final assembly to recall the activity of the last day or any day or years preceding. Millwrights already would have pulled down the overhead lines and removed the conveyors. A group of employee scavengers, some of them present at the last body drop, would zigzag in an eerie procession across the first floor from the sidesaddle area. They would move in irregular waves to all the metal disposal bins searching for discarded assembly line tools. The final assembly pit already would be stripped of tools and machinery. A women's bathroom door would have the words "door is locked, door is locked, door is locked forever" scratched on it. Several rat poison bait boxes would line the walls of final assembly.

But December 18, 1987, 10:53 a.m., one minute after the final body drop, the crowd was still cheering as they moved along the sides of the pit in order to trail the Fleetwood. They made room for the hood, fenders, and headlights installation. They buffed out all fingerprints with shirttails or the arms of blouses, smoothed the interior, and commented on the lights twinkling on the instrument panel after the battery installation. After the car passed all final inspections with flying colors, Santa Claus positioned herself behind it. Across her chest, she displayed a placard that read, ALL I WANT FOR CHRISTMAS IS MY JOB. Everyone fell in behind her. WKBX had switched on their lights long before the procession crawled the few feet past the headlight test station and the last under-hood inspection. Cameras rolled. The lady from the chassis line, who installed the right rear bumper shocks, strolled to the front in her red silk blouse and black wool skirt, nylons, and heels that she wore for the special occasion. She had tied a black band around her upper arm as so many others did that day. The general foreman of final assembly produced a tight smile to mask the noticeable furrow of sadness above his eyebrows. A couple of clerks from payroll stood by each other looking bewildered. Another lady from the chassis line broke ranks with the procession and stuck her head through the passenger window for one last look. Santa yanked her cap off and waved it back and forth. And a one, and a two, and na na naa naaaa. Na na naa naaaa. Hey-hey-hey . . . goooood-bye.

Manuel, Manuel Everywhere

As Manuel placed his foot on the curb to enter the main street of the annual Mexicantown Festival, a scent of lime and a cooking spice like cinnamon or clove tickled the hairs in his nose in competition with the delicious smell of *comino* and cilantro emanating from the La Taquería stand immediately to his right. Then he spotted the back of a woman sitting at one of the picnic tables set up for the festival. Juices from a *taquito* she was eating dribbled down her right arm. Amused, he continued observing her. The longer he watched her the more distinct was the scent of lime. By this time he was leaning on the edge of the taco stand. He looked over his shoulder to see if perhaps a bowl of lime was nearby. Seeing no lime, he turned his attention again to the woman. Something about her was familiar to him. It was the way her hair was piled on top of her head. Benny Cruz y la Buena Vida Band had finished tuning and the lead guitarist strummed a few chords to a song that must have been familiar to the woman, one that she liked because she swung her head to the right and smiled and gestured to someone in the distance. Then he recognized her as Rosario, a woman he had known at work. To think that after so many years he would see her here at this festival with red salsa around the edge of her mouth. He realized then that the smell of lime could only have come from her. Ah Rosario, where have you been?

It is, as they say, a long story that began years ago. When Manuel first saw Rosario Salazar she was working on the second floor in the body-wiring group near the stairs to the medical department. He watched her slide in and out of the center of each car's front seat to install the radio bezel. The day was hot outside and like a furnace inside. It was like hell for her, being in the airless cars with their temporary plastic protective seat covers. When she emerged from each car, Manuel saw the sweat streaming down her face. Such a beautiful face, smooth and olive, round with large round eyes. *¡Qué mujer!* Her hair was wrapped around her head several times; it would have been impossible to move through the car with waist-length hair. She replenished screws and decorative stickers in her short work apron with a peaceful half smile on her face. As she looked down to gather her stock her eyes appeared closed. What an angel, so innocent and sweet. And then whenever she exited a car, Manuel would get a whiff of her perfume, a smell like cloves, lime, and another ingredient that reminded him of being in church, and the rapture he would feel there sometimes as a child when the choir sang and he looked up and all he could see were angels and stars hovering above him. *¡Qué mujer!* He wondered at the strength of her odor because in the factory usually you were overwhelmed by the smell of manufacturing oils mixed with old, shaved steel.

Manuel fell in love then and there, after observing her for only five cars, just before her break when he saw her walk to the beverage machine. Her body was tiny, tiny. She was like a waif. Her delicate lips sucked the edge of the paper cup filled with cola. Manuel fell in love hard.

He fell so hard that he couldn't move a single muscle to go up to her, introduce himself, offer to treat her to lunch or even ask her name. Oh what do you do in a situation like that when confronted with a vision that comes from heaven and you want to talk to it? That was Manuel's predicament. So he came every day from his job on the first floor across the street in the block area to gaze at Rosario. He came twice a day on his breaks and followed her to lunch if she ate in the cafeteria, or if she ate at her work station he settled himself far enough away that he could observe her without being seen.

For her part Rosario didn't notice Manuel and his maneuvers. She was new in the factory, new in the United States, fresh from Agualeguas, Mexico, and in her head were dreams and dreams and dreams about how she was going to make it in this country. She had a sister here, but her sister had too many children and a bad marriage. Rosario herself was escaping a brutish husband in Agualeguas; her mother's death was her excuse to leave. She had noticed a cute young foreman in her department, the section after hers. She knew little English, but focused on communicating with him by oozing demureness, fluttering her eyes, and smiling.

One day Manuel intercepted a look like that meant for the foreman that Manuel thought was for him. Finally, he said to himself, she has noticed me. He was elated because prior to that glance there had been no indication from her that she knew Manuel existed.

Emboldened by Rosario's smile, Manuel walked over to her, waited until she exited the car she was working on, and began a conversation with her. Clumsily at first—How are you? It must be hot in the car? Do you drop many screws on the floor? Boy it's tough working on the line. You smell like heaven. What perfume are you wearing?

Nothing, no response from Rosario. A blank look, then her lips parted into a weak smile. She entered another car to install a bezel. Manuel stood in the same spot as she exited; he was no more than four or five inches from her face. Oh if I could kiss those lips, take her in my arms right then, right there in front of everyone. Declare her mine. She said to him, I don't know, in halting English. What did "I don't know" mean? Manuel wandered off perplexed asking himself over and over what "I don't know" meant. Was she in his head? Did she read his mind? Was she simply saying that she didn't understand English? The first words from her to him: I don't know.

He could have spoken Spanish to her, a few words of greeting. But his Spanish wasn't strong enough to speak sentences of love. He would sound stupid. Rather than make a bad impression, he preferred making no impression at all.

Manuel didn't return to that department until months later after the big 1974 layoff when he went in search of Rosario, wondering if she had survived the cuts. She was gone as were several others who had worked in that area. Those who were left informed Manuel of the whereabouts of the others: Joe went to first-floor final assembly, Mike to the sidesaddle, Raul to fifth-floor painting. Many who disappeared during the layoff resurfaced in other departments. Manuel searched out his *amigos* from first floor to fifth on final assembly side. He waved his hand and yelled *Wassup?* or *¿Qué pasa?* as he walked past familiar faces in unfamiliar spots, but he refused to think anymore about Rosario. He told himself that not finding her was a sign, time to move on with his life. No one mentioned her name or where she was working. Maybe she was reassigned to Plant Four on the east side of the city. Maybe she was tucked away in the Engineering Building; he couldn't gain entry there. Good. Maybe she was on afternoons in plastics, or in the cam department. No, there were no women there. Ah, maybe she was on afternoons in the same body wiring department.

Manuel developed reasons to stay over on afternoons. At first he told himself he was searching for an old friend, Joe, from whom he borrowed five dollars once. He wanted to repay him. When he found Joe in the paint department, Joe said that he had never borrowed money from him, but I'll take it Manny, if you have money to throw away.

Then Manuel volunteered to work double shifts as a plantwide spare man to fill in for afternoon absentees on the final assembly line, on the motor line, in Seville. On his afternoon shift breaks, Manuel walked. *Wassup?* he hollered to familiar faces on afternoons. *¿Qué pasa?* I'm working a double, man. Gonna buy me a Cadillac with this extra money. Manuel was everywhere, everywhere looking for Rosario without knowing himself that he was under the control of subconscious desires.

Manuel was the kind of person who functioned on autopilot ninety-nine percent of the time. Not that he was incapable of love; he just couldn't sit still long enough to nurture it. But Manuel was a sweet, sweet man. He left a spicy trail from his cologne even after a full shift. He showered in between shifts in order to stay sweet smelling. He never knew when he would run into Rosario although he refused to admit, even to himself, that he needed Rosario more than fish needed water. That was about the time that the women in the plant began calling him Sweet Manny. He thought to himself, oh if only I could get close enough to her we could form a tunnel of sweet spicy love in this crazy dirty stinking place.

His mother used to tell him when he left for work each morning, Manuel, you smell like a drugstore. In his own opinion, Manuel needed every bit of help he could muster to make him appealing to the women. At five feet three inches, he was looking up to some of the most beautiful women in the plant, except for Rosario. She was tiny, not even five feet. He towered over her. He could take her in his arms like a little doll and rock her and love her. Oh where was Rosario? If she could have seen the passion in his gray eyes. The eyes alone would have intrigued her. A Mexican with gray eyes. Maybe because of his light brown hair she didn't realize he was Mexican. Why didn't he take his shades off the day she stood so close to him? He would have had her then. Why didn't he speak a few words of Spanish to her? Why wasn't his Spanish better? Why didn't his parents speak it to the children at home? Why did he hang out with so many *güeros* when he was growing up? Why? Why?

That Manuel lost his spunk and began to blend into the rhythm of the factory can't be blamed entirely on his unrequited obsession with Rosario. He had, after all, been at Cadillac for five years. After that much time your body began to look like a factory body: a little dumpy, even if you were young. There was a tiredness that escaped as a constant sigh. You could hear it. Others could see it in the way you moved, like a bar of lead. The spirit began to lag naturally. Realism replaced optimism. Dreams became small: a wish for a break in the line, no union dues out of the next check, a fun week-end. There's no help for that. Except in Manuel's case, if he had found his Rosario in good time. If he could have continued to gaze at her even from a distance, maybe he would have continued to dream himself a bigger life with a beautiful woman at his side, a lovely home. Maybe one day the Cadillac, children in college. A white picket fence surrounding his home in the suburbs. A swimming pool.

By some miracle, Manuel's five years seniority was enough to keep him in the manufacturing building on the block line where he had worked from day one at Cadillac. He knew every job in that area, from block washing to honing. The block line was the base for his forays from one floor to another looking for what? Even he didn't know anymore. Up to the second-floor piston section, over to the Hub Building and the C-Five Dock. Next break: straight back to the salvage lot to shoot the breeze with Hook, the security guard, and the others who gathered in the greasy courtyard: Peanut Man with his hot roasteds, Dancing John, Ramón, Mario the hi-lo driver from line one, a long way from home that one. He always had stories about the women. Yeah, we got one on the line, now. Just came back from layoff. What a fine Mexican mama. Straight from the old country. Ooo if I could get to her. She came from across the street somewhere.

How many Mexican women could there be in that plant? Manuel cruised down the motor line during a lag in his job and couldn't believe his eyes. There was Rosario on the tim-ing-chain job, her head bent into the line as if she were con-versing with it. Her eyes, as usual, looked closed. Her face so serene. Ah, Rosario. It had been so long, Manuel couldn't remember what it was he wanted to tell her. Would you marry me? Would that be too forward? How about a date? He poofed his chest out, hitched up his pants, adjusted his shades for maximum suave effect, patted his long curly light brown hair into place, smelled his top lip to make sure he emitted only beautiful odors. Then, then he approached Rosario on the line. I see you made it back. That was it. That's what he told her. I see you made it back. But it was enough, because she looked him full in the face, smiled the smile of an angel, and said, Oh, I see you too, yes. They chat-ted about her layoff experience. When she was recalled she was shipped around to various departments before assign-ment to the motor line. How do you like the job? It's nice. The people? They are nice, too.

For several weeks, Manuel visited Rosario every day, twice a day, sometimes three times a day. He became established on her job in the way that men had of establishing themselves. At first he replenished her supply tray, loaded it up with the screws and star washers she used for the timing gear. Then when she placed the gear and chain on, he began inserting the two screws and washers. Next, he put the gear and chain on. Soon Manuel did the whole job and Rosario could take extra breaks. When she walked down the aisle to the ladies' room, all the women would give her sly looks, shake their hips, flip their eyebrows up and down as if to say, You've nabbed one. He's eligible. Go for it. Ah ha haaa they would sing out. Rosario would grin back at them sheepishly and keep walking.

Finally, the day came when Manuel felt that he had established himself enough. It was time to make his move. To push beyond motor line friendship. He asked her for a date: dinner, dancing, movies, whatever she wanted. No, she said, no. You're nice but no. There is someone else.

That was a crushing blow for Manuel. After weeks of careful preparation. For a whole year, something inside of him had fervently hoped he could have Rosario as his woman. He had brought her *pan de huevos* from La Gloria Bakery and tamales he made that Christmas with his mother and sisters. But, he said then to himself, when she told him no, that he had thought of no one else but her for a whole year. Ever since he had first laid eyes on her, she was the woman for him. Oh yes, there were dates with other women over the past year, he was a man after all and Rosario was still just a dream in his heart. Since he had been visiting her on the job, he had been cooling it with his other lady friends. There were a few others. He was a young single man, after all.

Manuel stopped visiting her immediately. His face wasn't seen in or near the motor line area for months even though his department was the next one over. He had his pride.

Everyone knew that he had been hot for Rosario. It would be clear to everyone that she had rejected him. He couldn't face her anymore. His friends asked him why he wasn't visiting that cute little gal on line one anymore and he said that she was messed up. Stuck on herself. Not his type. By that statement and the snap in his voice, the men knew that she had rejected him and no one mentioned Rosario again.

In the factory, time passes like a thief. Before you know it you are someone else, unrecognizable from the person who entered the factory world so many years before. This is true of life on the outside as well, but in the factory you have a peculiar sense of never seeing daylight. You are so immersed in gray that even on sunny days off, somewhere inside of you, things don't seem normal. You feel as if you should be back in the hole. Time passes like a gray thief, slinking from one moment to the next, stealing pieces of everyone.

It stole something from Manuel. It was time that stole Manuel's optimism, not Rosario. In place of optimism, time left a few pounds. Manuel grew a little chunkier and to his surprise so did Rosario. The next time he saw her was at Lolita's, a neighborhood lounge. He was there with some friends. He never figured her for a lounge type, but there she was celebrating her divorce with a few girlfriends. They danced, and he slipped her his phone number. She never called.

On the summer evening he drove from his home in a Detroit suburb to the barrio for the festival he was restless again. He cruised up and down Vernor then Porter then circled Clark Park. He automatically drove down Clark Street to the plant. Then he decided to ride by the plant to see who he could find. Maybe Hook would be there working a double shift. Maybe Raul or Mario. By this time he had been working at the General Motors Livonia Engine Plant for several years. He hadn't seen many of his friends from downtown in ages. He drove down Clark Street with the laughter of the children in the park and the rhythm of the salsa music from the cassette tape vendor on the corner of Vernor and Clark ringing in his ears. The further he drove into the complex, the quieter things got. He hadn't been in the vicinity of the plant on afternoons since final assembly closed. There was no one working on that shift except a few guards and a few people in engineering. He thought about the hundreds of people who used to be out on Clark Street at just that hour having lunch, drinking beer out of brown paper bags. They sat on the steps of the administration building and along its ledges. On afternoons, there were no big shots to care about where anyone sat on a summer evening at lunch. Down the street in the salvage area people sat in the courtyard, on the ledge in front of medical. As Manuel continued his drive down Clark Street on that summer evening there was no one sitting anywhere.

Then he stopped in front of medical across the street from the salvage area. Maybe that is where Hook is, he thought. To his surprise, a demolition ball dangled in the air in the salvage area and there were bricks already in a heap. The area was barely recognizable. The demolition of salvage had begun that day; the demolition ball had taken its first swing without his knowledge.

It was then, right then, that Manuel felt the first slow moment in his life. His mouth hung open; his breathing became deep and loud. His eyes became as wide as the lenses on his glasses.

The courtyard had encompassed the area outside of manufacturing and the actual salvage building. It wasn't a courtyard, really, but it functioned as a gathering place, outside of the building but on the grounds. It was a place where you were out but still in during the official work hours when no one was allowed to leave the building, unless it was job related. So the courtyard held a special fascination for Manuel, who had spent many pleasant times in the area. He stood for a long time wondering if it had all been a dream. It looked then to him as if the salvage area had never existed.

In a state of shock at the changes in the place where he had spent over twenty years of his life, Manuel eventually found his way to the festival on Bagley. There was Rosario sitting at the picnic table listening to the music of the La Buena Vida Band. He had been standing in the shadows of the *taquería* stand observing her. It had been a long time, and this was what he was accustomed to, observing her from a distance. Suddenly she looked up and recognized him immediately. *¡Hola!,* she cried out and threw her arms open as if to hug him. He stuffed his hands in his jeans and straddled over to her, already formulating what he would say. He would ask her if she wanted more to eat, if she would like a *cerveza.* Then he would ask her to dance with him, and as they danced he would breathe her perfume and maybe he would brush away a lock of hair from her face. It was always so like her to have long strands of hair dangling around her eyebrows, getting caught in her mouth. Yes, they would dance; the band was playing the beautiful *"Quiéreme Mucho."* He could whisper in her ear the words of the song, *Qué amante, siempre te adoré.* Then after they danced he would ask her how her life had been since the old days, and they would spend the rest of the evening laughing and dancing.

We Have a Job for You

Hegel remarks somewhere that all great, world-historical facts
and personages occur, as it were, twice. He has forgotten to add:
the first time as tragedy, the second as farce.

—KARL MARX, *The Eighteenth Brumaire of Louis Bonaparte*

One by one they descend from the Michigan Avenue bus at
Clark Street by a grotto of blue and white steel signs pro-
claiming CADILLAC DETROIT HEADQUARTERS. Moderately bun-
dled for November, they follow the curve down Clark to the
interior of the complex as if they belong there, a man then a
woman, a woman then a man, the dark brown, tan, or near-
white of their skins barely discernible in the predawn darkness. Some stump close to the curb; some advance straight-
backed in the middle of the sidewalk. A few head confidently
toward a grayish brown security cubicle just outside a parking
lot gate fashioned from black wrought iron and the cadmium-
colored bricks salvaged from the old West Assembly Building.
The guard station is unoccupied, the gate locked. So they

press on with the others, compelled by the wisp of smoke issuing from the powerhouse located where the curve ends. A few feet more and they are at the next guard shack in front of a courtyard enclosed by another wrought iron fence.

—S'cuse me, sir, can you tell us where the employment office might be?

Those who enter the complex from the barrio end of Clark Street where it intersects Vernor Avenue march up past the burnt-out houses that are Cadillac's immediate neighbors, march past Cadillac's waste treatment plant on one side of the street and the Craftsman Credit Union on the other, over Cadillac's railroad tracks, and past Cadillac's administration building, marbleized by a mix of warm and cold grays, until they arrive at the same guard shack. —Can you tell us where they're hiring at?

Hook, the security guard on duty, nods his head indicating the door across the street from his cubicle, EMPLOYMENT OFFICE, SECURITY, LABOR RELATIONS.

Cars come, too, loaded with people. Raggedy heaps, inner-city blues zigzagging to the curb by every door. Heads poke out to glean information from the doors and pull back in when they spot nothing. They see the elegant granite sign with raised black lettering announcing CADILLAC ADMINISTRA- TION WORLD HEADQUARTERS, but the columns of black windows the sign references reveal no interior lights, no motion in the lobby. Finally, they arrive at Hook's station where he rolls his eyes and says, —See that door, man? Two or three, three or four climb out of the cars and their sleepy, snaggletoothed drivers squeal away.

Hook watches, fascinated by the ghostlike figures situating themselves one by one at the employment office door. At first he thinks they are displaced Cadillac workers, job bankers waiting for reassignment. Perhaps they are here because plating, the only production operation remaining, is scheduled to discontinue in the spring. Slowly he realizes that these are not Cadillac workers. There are too many of them and none are familiar to him. He calls the captain of security at the command post which overlooks the door where the people are queuing. —Man, is Cadillac hiring?

At the south end of Clark on the second floor of the manufacturing building, Bill Bowling is aroused by the sudden rumbling of a machine or fan somewhere near. He raises his bulbous head from the crook of his left arm in response and curses the dim overhead light that sears his eyes, sensitized by Jack Daniel's. This has been a pattern lately, weekends spent at union functions and political gatherings in search of a useful retirement position. He crawls into the plant Sundays at midnight to sleep in his gravy-stained union shirt, guaranteed to be on time for work Monday thanks to Hook, who knows that after years of gadding about for the union, Bowling has no real home life with his wife. And now he faces retirement.

Bowling attempts to separate his upper torso from its sprawl on the picnic bench where cleaners, sweepers, and hi-lo drivers gather daily in shifts to play poker, gin rummy, and spades. He is jerked back down when both pockets of his union blue shirt catch on the edge of the table. No wonder. They are stuffed with the kind of paraphernalia that passes for union steward gear: small pads of paper, a couple of pens, an open pack of cigarettes in one pocket and an unopened one in the other, a vinyl-covered book that looks like a date agenda, a couple of pipe cleaners, and a comb. Once he extricates himself from the grip of the table, he stretches his 1927 frame, freeing his shirt pockets to bulge front and center, two large protrusions hanging like size D breasts. His shirt strains to fit the many curves and protuberances of his body; its buttons pop to accommodate his belly and the fleshiness of his sides.

—You've come a long way baby, he hums.

He has spent many days lately recovering from drinking binges at this table. After thirty-six years at Cadillac, the prospect of retiring weighs heavily on him. He has walked the four- and five-story Cadillac production buildings almost daily as a committeeman and as the consummate union politician. The buildings are his life, even though he no longer has a union position. But he sees the writing scrawled on the wall. With the closing of plating in a few months, he will join a merry scramble for the few remaining easy stock and cleaning jobs available. This is not the way he envisioned spending his golden years of in-plant retirement, the time when he should saunter through the facilities as if he owned them because he has paid his dues.

When he hired in, his café-au-lait skin and slicked-down curly hair landed him an easy job on the c-five shipping and receiving dock. This was at a time when most blacks were stuck in the hot foundry. In his reveries these days, he recalls faces but not names, incidents but not dates. One incident that is still vivid in his memory, to the exact day and hour, occurred on Thursday morning, March 3, 1955, one week after he hired in.

Back then, the Ku Klux Klan held open meetings at the plant and blacks were not even allowed to sweep near the assembly lines. A white dock worker named Joby, reputed to be a member of the Klan, made the mistake that morning of grabbing Bowling by his balls while he was bent over moving some stock. Bowling laughs now as he remembers that some of the white men in the plant then would grab a black's testicles to check for size, confirm the myth. He knew that was on Joby's mind because as he approached Bowling from the rear, he said, —Well, boy, let me see if you light-skinned ones are just as big.

It is the same in the factory as in the rest of life: reality and hope often mix in such a way that new motivating truths emerge. That was the case with the punch from Bowling's fist that landed on Joby's jaw. Joby was so stunned that his first attempt at ball-squeezing had met with resistance that, from then on, he confined his harassment of the blacks to name-calling. The older men, who had encouraged Joby to grab Bowling, were so surprised that Bowling had taken such immediate and decisive action with no other blacks around for support that they never reported the incident to management, who would have fired Bowling on the spot. The blacks, who that day heard about the incident through the grapevine, were so pleased to have a wild, no-shit-taking nigger in their midst that they launched Bowling's political career at the plant that evening at a hastily called meeting at someone's house, Bowling can't remember whose, by making him honorary president of the Cadillac Flower Club, a self-help organization established among the black foundry workers.

Over the years, Bowling's role in the political life of the plant grew to such an extent that he became Mr. Cadillac even to the white and Latino workers. He was at the forefront of forcing slots for blacks in the local union hierarchy. He eventually held several union positions himself: committeeman, recreation chairman, elections chairman. A banquet here, a cabaret there, this picket line, that picket line, union meetings, election campaigns. Bowling was the union.

Now he is on a personal campaign to secure a job at Solidarity House; a financially secure retirement from the plant hinges on a paying job there. His campaign has taken him to every UAW dinner and cocktail gathering within the tri-county area. Although he is already on a first-name basis with almost everyone of importance, Bowling needs to show-case his longevity and energy, his useful combination of his-tory and vitality.

—Remember the good old days? Bowling pumps the hand of the head of the UAW. —Those were the days in the trenches. And to his regional director, who was born the year Bowling hired in at Cadillac, —We had some battles back then. Sometimes Bowling loses track of who he is talking to after a few drinks, in the smoky air, and one conversation melts into another.

Bowling sighs as he kicks his legs, first the right then the left, to see if they still work. He begins his customary walk toward Hook's station to shake off the effects of last night's fundraiser. From his location he spots a few stragglers trudg-ing up Clark Street from Vernor toward the employment office, but he is unaware that they are the tail end of the mass further up.

Patsi Wheeler, the salary coordinator for the skilled trades apprenticeship program, sees a few bodies wandering on Scotten Street, the back of the plant, but she dismisses them as Engineering Building employees. She crosses through the viaduct from the tri-level structure where she parks to the final assembly building. Her office is located there on the sec-ond floor, down the hall from the security command post. She has passed through that viaduct over Scotten Avenue for ten years. She is a young woman with bright red hair and green eyes that usually smile as she enters the viaduct and greets the security person. But today there is no smile as she begins her last week of crossings. Then she, like those who did not survive the 1987 car assembly shutdown, and those who will not survive the upcoming plating closure, will hit the unemployment office until she can find another job. This week she will finish her work of processing minority applications for skilled trades apprenticeships. Because General Motors is under their quota for minority and women apprentices, she has been conducting special orientations and testings to bolster the numbers. —How ironic, she thinks. I am training those who might get a job. Where is mine?

There is no happy clop clopping of her basic black heels this morning. She walks slowly and counts her steps as if she can prolong the inevitable. She multiplies her steps by four for the four days remaining on the job, then doubles that amount because she will return to her car at the end of each day by recrossing the viaduct. Then she adds one more viaduct crossing because at the end of this day she will return to the car. No point in counting crossings for lunch excursions. There have been none since she received the pink slip a week ago. Patsi stops at the end of the viaduct to do the mental calculations and comes up with a ridiculous figure she rounds off to a million steps. —I have a million steps left, to and fro.

The confident, determined posture of the crowd at the employment door earlier melts to an uncomfortable shuffling as a wayward sliver of dawn sneaks onto Cadillac's main street, revealing a complex of brewery-clean, red oxide factory buildings. Where is the grime and grease of auto production? It will be a gray day—a factory gray day, leaden, thick, dreary. The kind that dawns and sets without a noon. Dirty clouds are lured between the production buildings and trapped there blocking the sun. By the railroad tracks over what is called lower Clark, a three-story viaduct connects the old manufacturing engine building to the final car assembly building. Its light royal blue paint, known as Cadillac blue on Clark Street, provides a kind of sky for Cadillac workers. There is a rectangular sign exactly in the middle of both sides of the viaduct. The sign, the same as the signs at the bus stop and on the warehouse building, has three squares: the Cadillac crest on the left, the word CADILLAC scribed in logo form in the middle, and a white, boxy GM on a marine blue background to the right. Underneath, the words Buick, Oldsmobile, Cadillac reflect the latest General Motors organizing scheme.

The design of the crest, which is located at all major points on Clark Street and on the hood ornament of every Cadillac car, was developed from the coat of arms of the de la Mothe Cadillac family, one of the most ancient families of France, the family that spawned Antoine, the founder of Detroit. Branches of the de la Mothe family fought the Holy Crusades under this coat of arms with its merlette birds recalling the Trinity, and its squiggly lines representing feudal property.

The entire banner on the viaduct at the lower end of Clark evokes the days when Cadillac was in full production, when Antoine's family coat of arms and the words, CRAFTSMANSHIP A CREED AND ACCURACY A LAW dominated that end of Clark.

Midway on the street, another viaduct connects the administration building to offices on the third floor of the manufacturing building. It is a two-story structure with black, sun-shielding glass. A large Cadillac crest, enclosed by a square, hangs on either side centered on the viaduct but not on the street. Because the administration building is set back further from the sidewalk than the manufacturing building, the crest hovers over the street off-center, as if in defiance of the craftsmanship creed.

As the crowd waits for the employment office to open, they are everywhere surrounded by crests and banners reminding them they are in Cadillac territory. But they are veterans accustomed to territories in the car wars. They have maps of Detroit factories etched on their faces. Somewhere on their persons they have the souvenirs from each of their previous jobs. There are hats in the crowd with the blue Ford oval or the silver Chrysler star with BUY AMERICAN arced over it. Others wear jackets bearing the specific emblem of Pontiac, Chevrolet, Buick, or Oldsmobile, branches of the General Motors family. Some jackets sport the UAW circle of hands and the name of an in-plant caucus, the Action Group, for example, a reminder of hopes for internal union reform. Now they come to join the Cadillac family working under Antoine's crest.

Patsi's family was in a mess when she entered Cadillac eight years ago, she and her three children abandoned by an alcoholic husband. A fortunate encounter with a Cadillac union representative landed her a job as a third-level office clerk, an odd way to enter the factory, as a salaried worker through a union connection. Leakage of this information along with her almost meteoric rise to her current sixth-level position prompted speculations by her coworkers.

Too fast, they whispered. She moves too fast.

The minority salaried workers used her as an example of the power of the white girl. Many of her peers, white, black, and Latino began calling her Wheeler Dealer behind her back and sometimes in front of her face.

After one time comes another. Because of the reduction of plant operations, all of her detractors have moved to other locations or are furloughed. What did they know about how hard she worked in order to support her children? In the factory everyone creates their own reality and her coworkers drummed up a loose and sex-driven one for her. None of what they thought or what she did makes any difference now, thinks Patsi, as she reaches in her dress pocket to touch the pink slip she has carried with her every day since she received it. As she nears the hallway to her office, the captain of security meets her and asks, "Is Cadillac hiring?"

At the fundraiser for a lady running for a judgeship, Bowling found himself in vigorous union pump-handshakes with almost everyone at the function, union leadership and hacks alike as well as community leaders. Enthusiasm for a woman judge could identify him as progressive, able to keep up with the times.

In the process of glad-handing the fiery and influential pastor of New Mount Moriah Missionary Baptist Church, Reverend Jules Hicks, Bowling let slip that a few apprenticeships might be available at General Motors for minorities. Bowling himself had heard that whisper in the local union hall as it passed from a committeeperson to the vice president. Bowling offered the information to Reverend Hicks because he had a fierce, earnest look on his face when he asked Bowling, "What is the union going to do about jobs, brother, what is the union going to do about jobs?"

Bowling has such an extensive and colorful history at the plant that he considers himself a prime mover. So when Reverend Hicks asked, What is to be done? Bowling felt a rush of pride and importance as he responded, "Call me at the union hall Monday."

Reverend Hicks is a preacher, not a factory man. He knows nothing about the difference between an apprenticeship into an automotive skilled trade and unskilled factory work. Jobs are available, that's what he heard Bowling say. His sermon the next morning is about finding beauty in the trash heaps of forgotten souls in the city, in the country, in the world. As the sermon dances and sings its way to a crescendo, his personal agony rushes to the surface and pushes his voice to new levels of pleading. He recalls all the troubles he has been experiencing operating a church in the middle of a crack-infested neighborhood, the break-ins, the loss of membership because of fear, the increasing jingling sounds in the collection box. All of these problems wiggle their way into the Reverend's heart as he delivers the homily. But being a man of the cloth, the more he prays and invokes the name of the Lord, the more his sermon turns toward hope. He begins to speak of moonbeams of happiness and salvation, riches and security floating on the waves of his message directly from the Lord, through his soul to that of his congregation.

Brothers and Sisters, the Lord came to me last night in the form of a man from the Cadillac plant. He said there is a job for you. And the Reverend takes a deep suck of breath that rivets the upturned faces, browns against the blond varnish of the semicircle of pews and the pulpit. Each of the fifty members that morning in a church with a capacity for three hundred watch the sweep of Reverend Hick's maroon-robed arm.

Yes, Brothers and Sisters, there is a job for you building those big, bright shiny Cadillac cars and you will be in the driver's seat of life again. There is hope, there is hope. We have a job for you. And he gave a whoop. Aaeeeeiiii!

Hook scans his morning paper in hopes of finding the reason for the single-file line of people that begins at the employment office door and winds like a snake up and down Clark. In 1977, when job seekers crammed Clark Street, they were responding to a newspaper report. In the course of analyzing the status of the post-oil crisis auto industry, the article casually mentioned that manufacturers of "gas guzzlers" such as the Cadillac were confident enough in recovery to recall those on layoff and hire new workers. Hook never actually read the article but the reality of 5,000 people jamming every inch of Clark Street and sporadically fighting that September morning was proof enough that the newspaper was to blame. While workers inside the plant fabricated, painted, tested, and repaired the fabulous Cadillac cars that were in the first year of downsizing, police helicopters circled Clark Street blaring instructions to the restless hordes. —Go home, there are no jobs for you. Go home.

Workers who were not trapped on the line during the "riot of '77," hung out of the windows issuing encouragement to those outside. Keep on trying, there's a place for you in here. Hang in there; we made it, you can make it, too. Hook was called in along with other afternoon guards to beef up the Cadillac force. His first job was to retrieve the new head of the employment office from a phone booth outside of Hygrade's Restaurant on Michigan Avenue south of the plant. It was her first day and she was unable to report to the office because of the riot. Hook suffered jibes and barbs from the other guards, white and black, for escorting a white woman to the plant. His response then was the same as it would be now, a smile and then his back.

After retrieving the new employment manager, Hook was assigned to patrol the inside of the plant while the city police quelled the disturbance outside. The situation inside the plant required delicate handling because many of the rioters outside were related to workers inside. Any heavy-handedness by the police could have resulted in work stoppages or sabotage.

Hook was a perfect guard to circulate inside. He was a big man, six feet five and shoulders that seem broad as the 1977 Fleetwood Brougham was wide, with a smile as flashy as its chrome grill. He always sported the same short, salt and pepper afro. Hook was noted for prefacing and punctuating everything he says with the word "man." With this conversational peculiarity, Hook fit in perfectly with all the men, but he had great difficulty communicating with women. For this reason, his conversations with them were limited to grunts, nods, and smiles. With his height and big frame all he ever needed to do was smile, nod his head, and gesture, which is what he basically did the day of the employment riot. The burliest welders from third-floor manufacturing pulled their heads in from the grimy windows with a simple pat on the side from Hook and a "Come on, man."

Hook remembered hearing that some union reps, among them his friend Bowling, were selling applications to those in the crowd they could reach from a final assembly second-floor window. An application would travel down and something green would travel up. Hook asked Bowling if there was any truth to the rumor. Bowling said he handed out applications, but only to cousins he had told to come down and apply. Hook said, "But people saw money come your way, man." Bowling defended himself, "They paid me back money I loaned them." Hook never determined how Bowling and the others obtained the applications in the first place. It was one of those times when real truth was caught up and twisted in events until it became unrecognizable. In 1977 there were some jobs, a handful of them for the relatives and friends of management and the few union representatives and workers who were close to management. Cadillac had always been a family plant that hired the sons, daughters, and cousins of its employees. Hook knew that on the face of things it was absurd to think Cadillac would be hiring now, but who ever knows if that same principle isn't operating today as he watches the line of people become increasingly restless. Who knows?

They see the merlettes on the Cadillac crest on the two viaducts and mistake them for ducks. A trinity of the legless, beakless birds appears on the first and fourth quarterings of the Cadillac crest, father, son, and holy ghost to remind the knights of the Holy Grail of their sacred mission. They see the merlettes as they line up in the early morning gray, in single file along the outside wall of the final assembly building beginning at the employment office door, past the medical entrance, beyond the administration building, down to the railroad tracks, across the street and back up again until the tail of the line goes beyond the guard shack and disappears at Michigan Avenue. A young man, fifth in line, tired of waiting, tired of staring at the off-center crest on the viaduct suddenly blurts out, "Ducks, I'll be damned." Then they all look up, the faces from New Mount Moriah Missionary Baptist Church, their cousins, the friends of their cousins, cousins of their friends' cousins, *amigos* and *freunde*, *paisanos* and *przyjaciele*, friends of friends, all look up. Over from where the words CADILLAC MOTOR CAR COMPANY are etched onto the top of fourth-story manufacturing they see a gold crown atop a red, blue, and gold crest with solid black merlette trinities on the building's corner directly across from the employment office. It occurs to the young man, fifth in line, that there are an awful lot of ducks on Clark Street, and he quacks loud and laughs. Someone a couple of bodies behind him picks up on the joke and quacks a few more times, nasally. Another quacks in the form of the song, "Take Me Out to the Ball Game," and begins to waddle from side to side as if web-footed. Here a quack, there a quack, soon all are quacking. Quack, quack, quack, quack, quack, quack. Steady, insistent. The waddling becomes a march in place. Right, left, right, left. Quack, quack, quack, quack.

By this time Bowling arrives in Hook's guard shack and finds him staring in disbelief at the quacking people. "Bowling, man, look at this here."

Bowling scans the street, as much as he can see from the shack, and asks Hook what is happening. Hook looks at his disheveled friend and a suspicion rises from deep inside of him. He asks Bowling in his coolest, lowest whisper, "You know something about this, man?"

"Nothing, not a thing," replies Bowling who in truth does not remember any of the finer details of the previous evening but now stands frozen, his mouth open in utter shock at the event taking place before his eyes.

The captain phones Patsi, the only employment office manager on site that morning, and tells her to come right away, things are looking ugly. "They're quacking. There must be hundreds of them out there."

Patsi runs to the security office and peers out of the window at the mass of people in the street. She cannot distinguish the crowd from the buildings. Their warm and cool grays, the red oxide and cadmium bricks, the grayish brown of the security shack with its flat brown trim, the brown, tan, and white faces all mesh in the early morning light into a liver brown, pulsing from side to side toward the center of the street. The pulsing motion of the crowd seeps into her body and she begins to sway side to side and hum. The captain insists that she make a decision. Will she interview them or not?

"What do you want me to do?" she asks the captain. "In a week I'll be joining them."

And in a movement that surprises the captain, the security crew in the office, and Patsi herself, she reaches in her pocket, retrieves the pink slip and throws it along with a kiss to the job seekers whose quacking has reached such a pitch that the seagulls, who frequent the river less than a quarter of a mile from the plant, begin to fly over the buildings, adding their caw caw cawing to the din.

Nothing falls fast in the dense environment of Clark Street. So it is that Patsi's pink layoff notice flutters on the edge of her kiss before beginning its slow descent from the security office window on the second floor of the final assembly building. Slowly, slowly it falls toward the upturned heads of the people who cease quacking when they see Patsi fling her hand out of the window. They wait, wait, wait for the message from her to reach the first hand that can grab it.

Hook and Bowling wait also and hope, hope, hope that the message is good.

AUTOPSY OF AN ENGINE

Down Dirty

(A voice mail message, August 23, 1993, Cadillac Motor Car Company, Engineering Building.)

Uh hello. This is Bob responding to your Friday voice mail. Heh, heh. I was away at the Big Fella's special meeting up north. He was trying to get all of us managers together in one room to see if we could iron some things out. I'm referring specifically to the problem of office space when we close up shop down here and transition to your neck of the woods. But I'm sure you know all about that. In fact, I expected to see you at the meeting, but your former boss, who is now up at Pontiac—or did I get that confused? Are you originally from Pontiac?—anyway he told me that you were tied up with some issues from the meeting we had last week. The Tall One's session was quite a show. They had us holed up for two days in the resort. You know the one I mean. I'm sure you've been there. If you haven't you'll get there sooner or later. Sooner rather than later no doubt. It's beautiful in the summer. Outside the window of my room there were sunflowers big as large pizzas in a small garden loaded with black-eyed Susans and daisies yellow as pure butter. They just about blocked my view there were so many of them. Let's put it this way, they were my view. Heh, heh. Made my two days there seem brighter, though.

Well that's the gardener in me. Heh heh. Really, I'd guess that the Big Guy means to run us all through the love-ins before it's all over, if you know what I mean. In a way, I think it's good. I guess it's needed to get two entirely different organizations to march in step. You'd think we were two different auto companies the way they bicker in those meetings. Big Fella will put a stop to that. But you and me already got a few things straightened out on our own. If only the rest could be like us, eh? Heh, heh.

Well, I see you didn't waste any time in recharting the course for team 3D. Let me say this now because we didn't have a chance to talk personally when we got together last week to discuss the team, but I am convinced that you are the best man for the job. I know some people are going to want to make a big deal out of you taking over the reins of the team from me, but you are doing me a favor. Now I can concentrate more on the vision. You see the Big Guy's love-ins are already affecting me. What I mean to say is that we're all in this thing together; you know that old song *wherever you go, we'll go together* or something like that. Every last one of us has to chip in, find a squeaky gear, and oil it until this machine is running as smooth as honey on morning toast.

By the way, the bees up there were terrible. I swear some of them must have been those killer Brazilian bees. They didn't seem to want to take no for an answer, and I had the worst of it with all those sunflowers outside of my window. I'd wake up in the morning and bees would be bumping up against my window screen. I was going to advise you to make certain that you get scheduled for a meeting with the Big Guy in the summer, but on second thought you might want to shoot for the fall change of colors and avoid those bees. Northern Michigan change of colors can't be matched, and those bees can be killers. Got to look out for you old boy; it's all in your hands now.

Getting back to our meeting last week—I've been around here for a long time. Why I've probably been in a few dogfights around here that you haven't even heard of. Remember the decision to run the modular displacement engine for only one year? Of course you don't. You were at Pontiac then, weren't you? At any rate, you weren't downtown. How about Poletown, I mean Detroit/Hamtramck, you know, D/Ham, we're still suffering the aftereffects of that move. But I think we have one of the smoothest transitions of leadership on a transition team going. That sounds like I'm talking in circles, but do you remember all the stink around the change of guard on 4A? You and me, we got right down to business in our transition meeting defining the specific problem areas. That's what we need more of around here: the ability to define the problem. But then I guess it's easier when you have two good minds like ours hard at work. That's why I think that team 4D is on the road now. Sometimes it's easy to get lost in this mess. Here we are, talking about the transition of leadership on a transition team. We transition, the team transitions, all of our departments transition, the whole damn corporation transitions.

Well, in the middle of all these transitions let me just review briefly what we discussed in our meeting last week so that we don't lose our bearings and transition ourselves right out of the picture. Heh, heh. That's one of the techniques we learned this weekend with the Big Guy: create action bullet points and stay positive. So on that let me reiterate what we decided last week: I will, excuse me, YOU will sharpen the assignments on the one hand by broadening the application. By that I mean you will spread the work around to more shoulders. You will get specific about all matters pertaining to the move that impacts our team right down to the machinery and the footprints. If need be you'll delegate room by room. You'll call for daily updates on progress. The action bullet for that one is: contract in order to expand. I see that you've set September 17 as D-day for the final plan. I assume you discussed this with the team. I wasn't there because, as I said, I had to go up north with the Big Fella. Is everyone in agreement with that date? Does everyone think they can meet that deadline? Of course, I assume you have discussed that deadline with your boss out there. Of course you have; that's why they put you in charge. You know how to get the wheels rolling. Me, I'm an idea man. I'm still tinkering with the vision, but we've talked about that before. Without vision you can't see where you're going. Heh, heh. Whew that's a mouthful, good buddy.

These questions have been flopping around in my head since I got the word on the change of assignment. I wanted to make sure I got everything out. But one thing I'm not clear on is the down dirty idea that you stated on the voice mail you left me Friday. What you said specifically is that if we can't come up with a plan we'll have to go down dirty. Being the old codger that I am, I immediately had images of well, you know. You remember the time we all stopped into the topless bar after that meeting a month or so ago? Well, as soon as I heard down dirty on the voice mail I laughed because I still can't believe that you don't go for any of that stuff. Come on it's only for fun. You don't have to go home with any of them. Here we are in the semicircle booth; you're in the middle. Me and Fred slip her a twenty just so she could come over and dance for you, and she dances over our way. She wants you. You could see it in the way she looks straight at you and wiggles. She jumps on the table and dances right in front of you.

You should have seen the look on your face when we all scooted out of the booth and left you alone with all of that. Whooo, boy. I knew that down dirty didn't mean that, but I couldn't help thinking about that evening.

So just what do you mean by down dirty? It sounds like some kind of black thing, blues or something. Is that a buzz word or something you picked up from one of the sensitivity meetings? I never figured you for much of a blues man. Did you make that one up yourself? Down dirty. It sounds kind of cool, man. Heh, heh. Just getting into the swing of things. Cool, man, cool.

Actually, I've given down dirty some serious thought. You see the sunflowers are still in my mind. Something that beautiful, big, and raising its face to the sun has roots that go down deep into the dirt. Do we need to grow the business like those sunflowers? Down in the dirt. Down, down, down. So what does it mean, pal, down dirty? I've been working here for thirty-seven years. That's a lot of roots down in the dirt. After all these years I finally have come to realize that I am not more than I am. No, what I mean is that I have Texaco lube running in my veins. I'm every inch Cadillac. I guess I still hang on because I like fooling around with these hot rods.

Winter is the best time to go up north; bees won't buzz at all then, but then there won't be any sunflowers, just snow. Of course you won't be able to play golf. You know how the Big Fella is about golf. A lot of thorny issues get settled on the back nine. Gotta keep your head down back there. If you know what I mean. Of course, that's not the same as under the desk. Heh, heh. But they clear the roads off real good up there in the winter. You can get around better than you can down here. Of course, you won't have to worry about getting around. You'd be in sensitivity sessions all day long and in the bar at night. You could handle the bar up there. No girlies. The daytime bartender is a nice woman if you can sneak out during the day for a quick one. A drink I mean because she's just that, a nice woman. If there were any bees you wouldn't worry about them bumping up against your window screen because the window would be closed. It's too cold. What am I talking about? We need to grow this business, bees or not, sunflowers or not, in summer or winter.

Yeah, we're on a forced march, pal, but we can do it. Like they say it ain't over till the fat lady sings. I guess we know what that means, but what I've really learned from all these years in the trenches around here is that sometimes you gotta sing a little crooked. Heh, heh. Yeah, good buddy, sometimes you gotta sing a little crooked.

Autopsy of an Engine

This is how it is when she awakes from her travels. She has been to see the moon, a long journey from tip of star to tip of star. It leaves her breathless. She says to the moon: my nights are not long enough. The moon says to her: you ask for everything; you give me nothing. Not so, she tells the moon. I gave you lovely shiny red trinkets when I visited last night. The night before, I danced rumba for you on the back of a dog. Before that I gathered flowers and chased the rats from your doorstep. You have a habit of turning your cold back to me, she tells the moon. It is when you leave me in that way that I forget your glow.

The Chevrolet Engineering Motor Room is high-ceilinged with criss-crossing dirty beige beams, boxed fans, bright blue air hoses, and yellow electric chain falls with bulbous motors that dangle over strategic work areas like the fat asses of old women. It is a carnival of shapes and colors and fluorescent bright lights if you look above your head. If you look level, your eyes parallel to the floor, your head straight forward, you see a clutter of aluminum and cast-iron engines in various stages of being built or torn apart. There are red toolboxes, blue workbenches, blue cabinets called kits, which house the parts that are used to build engines by hand. Other cabinets house big scales, little scales, dial indicators, torque wrenches, pushers and pullers. Oil spots design the floor; you have only to lower your eyes to see them. And the room smells metallic in the areas where engines are built and like ashes in the teardown sections.

I am lost in this place. Like a stray seven-millimeter bolt under a bench. Like a used tie strap waiting on the floor to slip an unsuspecting foot. Like a cockroach. It's so big compared to Cadillac Engineering, where I started out before it closed and we were shifted to another General Motors location. Now more than ever I nestle in my work space, cling to my workbench. The space around it is my womb. In my womb there is always an aluminum Cadillac engine in some phase of disassembly. I have a card tacked to the bench with the picture of a blond woman and a brunette. It was a birthday message from a blond friend of mine. The card says we are not ditzy women. We are works of art. This is the vernacular of the motor room, the direct language of survival: I am not a bimbette, not a bitch. Understand that?

Do you understand that nearly every day I report to an operating room for steel where I dissect engines as if I were at the morgue autopsying a murder victim? A John or Jane Doe found in an alley? Although it's not fair to compare the engineering engines to abandoned bodies. The engines have after all been coddled, written about, studied, and killed in specific ways, on specific test schedules, on the Desert Proving Grounds, in sub-zero temperatures in Canada.

I can recite from memory the contents of my bright red toolboxes: the Snap-on box sits atop a PROTO roller-wheeled bottom box. I can tell you exactly what goes where from the top row of small drawers in the Snap-on to the last space in the PROTO.

In the Snap-on, I keep my check stubs and Band-Aids. Four small drawers hold my drills, taps, and an easy-out kit for when I fuck up and break a screw or bolt in a part. Four drawers run the width of the box and hold ratchets and wrenches, pullers and installers. There are hammers, pry bars and breaker bars, a self-made three-eighths-drive spinner and an extensive collection of files: itty-bitty fine ones and large raspy ones.

The men I work with make me things. One of the drawers contains a pretty little saw-blade holder with a pale green handle covered with plastic, a beautiful steel etcher with a brass screw-on top, and a three-eighths-drive, three-inch ratchet, very handy for tight spots. I wear the brass belt buckle with my name on it flap side on the right as a man would. The King Pleasure album is at home.

All of my electrical equipment stays in the PROTO, including an assortment of butt splices in one Nivea jar and every value of fuse known to auto humankind in another. I also keep my impact there. The final space in the bottom box is a deep catchall with a flip-out lid. I keep a box assortment of odds and ends there, as well as whiskey, rum, and wine bottles.

Should I go on? What's the use? It's true. I know more about the range of sockets in the top box, the screwdrivers, the ratchets, the Allen wrenches than I do about what is on this paper. I remember who I am by opening drawers and finding a wrench or a hacksaw. By smelling the musty sock odor from tools coated with dirty oil or stale gasoline and locked in the Snap-on and PROTO boxes over the weekends, over the holidays, over the years. By the feel of a knurled ratchet handle in the palm of my hand.

How easy for me to stare at a wrench for a long time and it becomes a ballerina. I learned that from my daughter, who can turn a pencil into an old woman, a pan into a condominium, a rock into an infant. She can devise all manner of tragedy and comedy with actors she finds in trash cans or under the couch.

I know you wouldn't believe me even if I were to tell you how terribly frustrated I have been the past few days struggling to fix my car, a raggedy heap of inner-city blues. It's a simple problem, apparently gone berserk because of an even simpler problem. Layer upon layer of engine mystery. I uncover one and another emerges. After seventeen years in the business each time I approach a car it is as if I know nothing, as if I barely know steering wheel from axle, distributor from throttle body, oil dipstick from oxygen sensor.

Oh, how helpless I feel when I raise the hood. Ugly demons merrily await the opportunity to nibble away at my ego. In the same manner I boot up the computer to write this story, for example, and I am a fumbling mechanic. I find myself raising a car hood when I begin a story. Who knows what lurks, greasy and rusted?

So, when it is me at midnight in the motor room, I am relieved to face an engine not under a car hood, but on its stand, waiting for my dissecting touch. It is then that she looks like a gypsy lady, buxom and flirty with hands on her hips. There is a certain point after I have stripped her of dress items—the air-conditioning unit, the alternator, the wiring harness, fuel rail, and so on—that she looks young and fresh, eager and willing for what I don't know. This is when I take pictures of her; it is required by the engineering teardown process. There is an eerie glow in my work area because I am located in a suburb of the motor room, the recipient of feeble rays from main-aisle lighting, dependent on the small fluorescent light on my bench.

Already you can see I am slipping into my imagination by calling the engine a she. Men do that all the time. They refer to their cars in the feminine. What man admits to riding him? It is the old girl who gives out. It is she who gets him to work every day on autopilot, faithful. What a gal.

So, on this night I have a gal too. I feel sad to see her exposed like that, me photographing her as if she were an old whore. I identify with her, yes. When I remove her front cover I can see the extent of damage, the wear on the timing chains. Cavitation on the gears. A light golden varnish on the oil pump.

I hate making obvious metaphors, a used engine and an older woman. I never would have thought about this until one particular engine. I saw patches of red along the cold gray lips of the intake ports on the right and left heads. I looked at my fingers then my hands for a gash that could identify the red as my blood. I found no cuts; then again the red was too pale, like fruit punch. Yet, against the gray dimpled aluminum in the eerie, midnight motor room light, the red looked like blood. I twisted my head this way and that. The engine swirled, as I did, round and round. Still, I was no more intelligent about the red patches. I remember the times when I worked on the assembly line many years ago that the sight of blood on an engine was cause for hooting and howling: *the blood of the workers. We are in a war.*

When I was seven years old and immersed in Catholic and spiritual Holy Communion days, I fell and scraped my right knee. Badly. For a few seconds after the fall no blood appeared. I gazed at the silver-dollar-sized patch of white as I fingered the flap of skin dangling by no more than an eighth of an inch connection to my knee. White, pure white. Not a capillary bubbled. Not a smudge of dirt from the fall mingled with the slimy dermis. I was looking at my soul, you know, lily white and mystifyingly accessible. Right there on my knee. Not inside of my chest as I had figured because of the rantings of the Catholic nuns and stern priests of my school. Not that they said the soul resides in the chest, but where else could a soul nestle safely but next to the heart, well-protected by chest bones? Except when you discover your soul on your knee one summer day on the large front lawn of your parents' home.

Or on the heads of a Northstar engine at midnight. I don't feel at war now, not in the quiet of midnight when only a few other people shuffle around. Some to measure engines, some to build them. I rip engines open during the night when if wolves could howl they would. I say a prayer for each piston I remove. One flops over in my hand, and I jump, startled. I remind myself this is aluminum and steel I am holding, not flesh.

I see no red on the pistons, none on the oil pick-up, and none on the fuel rails. I begin the scientific process. What could be red on an engine? Transmission fluid? Has the engine hemorrhaged, sucked up one of its vital fluids and gagged? So I sniff along the edges of the intake ports, but I smell nothing except the burnt carbon funk of old used engine. I pass the tip of my index finger along a lip of a port and wipe up a bit of the red fluid. It's greasy. I wipe it on my left wrist. It becomes brown like me.

The eye of Isis shines on her as she stands at the river. Birds flutter in her hair because it reminds them of the leaves of soft trees, but her hair is the color of an autumn moon. Already the sun dances on her face in the form of gold rings, and dots of diamonds shimmer from her nose, earlobes, and cheeks. From her outstretched arms fringes of rainbow flutter this way and that in the early dawn air. The air is too sleepy to make a commotion with the fringes. It is also too sleepy to carry her prayer to the heavens. To no goddess in particular for she has become accustomed to sending her wishes to the heavens on the tips of stars. Once a fervent prayer for her mother's health bounced off the moon. Silver threads of rays entered her mother's body and she was healed. Now she says all of her prayers from the main window of her mother's front room. The frogs jump in and out of that same window when the sun shines too brightly and they seek refuge in the kitchen behind a basin that is always filled with cool water.

You see how things can get away from you? Midnight in the motor room. I am completing the autopsy. The last set of parts I touch is the exhaust system. I shake the cross-under pipe for rattles; I look for holes. The cross-under is four inches across and curves like a stiff snake. It is easily cradled as I once cradled my son, then my daughter. I proceed to the exhaust manifold gaskets, flexing them back and forth, eyeing them for carbon leaks. I finger the joint where the donut seal fits on the Y-pipe. I extend the oxygen sensors and check for cracks in the wiring.

LOLITA HERNANDEZ

By this time, the palms of my hands are rust-colored and dusty. I am rusty-faced and exhausted. I will wait until the morning shift for the engineer's verdict on the red, but I have the unsettling feeling that things have gone too far, that I have begun to see more parts than the engineers intended in this engine and that there is no remedy for this, not even sleep.

Tomorrow night she will ask for a dream from whatever star or moon or galactic being will listen because it has been months since she has had one. Nights come, and she has no refuge in other worlds. No place to put her day. So she finds herself agitated and not well-rested. Her mother says: Make a tea of ginger; it will clear your stomach and open your mind. You will go to bed calm and happy like a baby. Your dreams will flow like the river. Her sister says: Bathe in the river an hour before bedtime under the light of the moon. The river water will soak into your pores and free the dreams from every cell in your body. A friend, who has a habit of dancing naked in the garden, says that she should lie on her back on the bank of the river facing the moon. If you keep your eyes open, no blinking, the moon will enter your body and direct your nights. Then you will dream.

FUNDER ACKNOWLEDGMENT

Coffee House Press is an independent nonprofit literary publisher. Our books are made possible through the generous support of grants and gifts from many foundations, corporate giving programs, individuals, and through state and federal support. This project received major funding from the National Endowment for the Arts, a federal agency. Coffee House Press has also received support from the Minnesota State Arts Board, through an appropriation by the Minnesota State Legislature and by the National Endowment for the Arts; and from the Elmer and Eleanor Andersen Foundation; the Buuck Family Foundation; the Bush Foundation; the Grotto Foundation; the Lerner Family Foundation; the McKnight Foundation; the Outagamie Foundation; the Pacific Foundation; the John and Beverly Rollwagen Foundation; the law firm of Schwegman, Lundberg, Woessner & Kluth, P.A.; Target, Marshall Field's, and Mervyn's with support from the Target Foundation; James R. Thorpe Foundation; West Group; the Woessner Freeman Foundation; and many individual donors.

This activity is made possible in part by a grant from the Minnesota State Arts Board, through an appropriation by the Minnesota State Legislature and a grant from the National Endowment for the Arts.

MINNESOTA
STATE ARTS BOARD

NATIONAL
ENDOWMENT
FOR THE ARTS

To you and our many readers across the country,
we send our thanks for your continuing support.

Good books are brewing at coffeehousepress.org